George Whitfield Hewes

Ballads of the War

George Whitfield Hewes

Ballads of the War

ISBN/EAN: 9783743300026

Manufactured in Europe, USA, Canada, Australia, Japa

Cover: Foto ©Andreas Hilbeck / pixelio.de

Manufactured and distributed by brebook publishing software (www.brebook.com)

George Whitfield Hewes

Ballads of the War

BALLADS OF THE WAR,

BY

GEORGE WHITFIELD HEWES.

NEW YORK:

Carleton, Publisher, 130 *Grand St.*

(LATE RUDD & CARLETON.)

MDCCCLXII.

CONTENTS.

PREFACE.

Busy times make busy men; if the bee would gather honey—the bee must be up and doing;—the river too, that would be the long and mighty, must accept all sizes and qualities of tributaries; for, having no ability either to refuse or choose, it must needs roll on, while every rivulet claims the right of companionship; and so, stirred by the times, and being unable to restrain my faculties when there was such volumes of hidden poetry in the many scenes now transpiring, I on August last, determined to do what I could to help along the great work of calling back the misguided and seceded brothers to the mighty family of States; to run my little voice in with the rolling thunder of an indignant people.

It is with no common solicitude that I venture before the public as an author, knowing as I do these poems to be the hard work of hours snatched from the taxations and relaxations of a mentally exhaustive profession; and it has been a doubt with me, whether they do not bear the marks of haste or feebleness, and as a consequence have been stamped with tameness; if such should be the fact, I beg the Public's pardon, and only promise to try and do better in future, or not to do at all.

Besides, we live in an uncommon time; uncommon events and feelings are to be celebrated, and here perhaps I can dovetail the thought, that an uncommon book would not be entirely out of place — at least I am determined to put on the front of boldness, and with an assumed " eye of Mars" show my face and my book together, compelling the public to beat me down into the mire (if sink I must) before I gracefully and tamely sink of my own weight; and in expanding this subject I will say, that if the public will hear me before they dismiss me, it will be as much as this attempt will justify, or my own ambition expect.

If it will be any extenuation of my presumption, to say that these poems were the production of an intense love of my country, an ardent hope that she may soon be restored to peace, and a sincere wish to extol the heroic deeds, extend the fame, and enwreath the memories of the soldiers who have fought and died for her, then indeed I am pardonable; for never had man a greater desire for the triumph of a cause, and to do honor to its votaries, than I have for the success of my country's rights, and her patriotic defenders. Let this be my palliation or my reward, just as the public censures or applauds.

Some may complain that these poems are not sufficiently warlike and descriptive in their character; that the great scenes of the present contest should so inspire the poet, that words of living flame should gush from his pen, even as the waters flowed from the great rock of Horeb, when smote by the hand of Moses. To such I must say, Firstly, that I have not the happiness to be a Moses; Secondly, there happens to be no thirsty multitude eager to sip at the bubbling fountain of my inkstand; and Thirdly, that I was unable, owing to my business arrangements, to visit any of the more prominent points of interest, by which I could fill my soul with the stirring scenes and sights of the war. I was compelled therefore to found my work upon incidents gleaned from the newspapers, or find in my imagination the foundation I so much needed and desired. I have chosen to blend the two as harmoniously as possible, but never have I perverted a fact. To create a fiction from a fact, is a work of the imagination, but, to coin a fiction and give it tacitly forth as a fact, is not only a deceit, but a crime, and deserving of the severest censure from the reading public. Imagination may assist reality by the vivid description of a great action; but it should never be allowed to control or pervert the facts belonging to it.

I do not herald these Poems as "the hasty occupation of idle moments, or "the result of an evening's amusement," they are the work of much labor and much love, and I do not care if the people know it. I am unwilling to cast a reflection on the taste of a reader by offering him a book "hastily prepared," and vainly blazoned to the public as a "thing easily done," when the reader's time could be more usefully employed in examining books of recognized ability. I may be presumptuous in bringing out my book, but I am neither impertinent nor

1 *

wilful. Poetry is not a mine that any one may shaft
and produce treasure, but rather a diamond sea in
which many divers are unsuccessful; and if I fail
this time in grasping the bright diamond of renown,
I shall but dive the deeper, and search the sea-clad
rocks the longer, until the crystal gem rewards my
persevering, but somewhat impatient industry.

But the critics! let me see! Is it well to address
them before they see me? I will however say, that
the book is theirs to handle as they please; for I do
not publish as an "experiment," but as a beginning,
(for other works may soon be on their hands if the
war does not kill them and myself off, before so de-
sirable a result is consummated.) Nor do I wish to
screen its defects behind a curtain of self inflicted,
derogating excuses in order to disarm them of any
severity they might choose to exercise. In my ef-
forts to be eloquent, I may have miscalculated my
ability; in my desire to exhibit and increase patriot-
ism, I may have overstepped the bounds of reason,
and produced nothing but illy timed and diseased
passion, but *I* do not think I have done so; and of
this I am certain, that I am sincere in my anxiety
to reverence sufficiently, and applaud discreetly, the
names and deeds of my fellow countrymen, and, in
my desire to sing their sacrificing love of principles,
to an admiring and appreciating posterity.

Encouraged by none, yet hoping this little book
may attain some of the purposes for which it is put
forth, the Author remains

The Public's humble servant,

G. W. H.

TO

THE MEMORY OF

THOSE HEROES OF THIS WAR

WHO HAVE FOUND A GRAVE IN THE TORN BOSOM OF THEIR COUNTRY,

AND TO THE GALLANT SOLDIERS

WHO ARE NOW SERVING HER,

This Book is Respectfully Dedicated

BY

THE AUTHOR.

BALLADS OF THE WAR.

THE BALLAD OF EVERARD GRAY.

'Twas night ; the moon in fitful rays,
　　Came gleaming the clouds between,
When through the smoothly gravelled walks
　　All shaded o'er with green,
I walked into a mad-house near,
　　And gazed upon a scene.

The wind sighed in and out the trees
　⁃ From many a boughy wreath,
And seemed to moan so tenderly,
　　It took away my breath ;
And struck a chord within my soul
　　That somehow told of death.

I gazed on the structure reared there
　　Whose massive columns blended
With the snowy white of the doorway,
　　As though they were intended
For the bridal train of beauty,
　　Of some Lordly mansion splendid.

And instead of the festive group
  I saw but the glaring eyes,
Pressed hard against the barrèd light
  That opened to the skies,
Whose strength the howling lunatic
  Each night so vainly tries.

Instead of the rustling dresses,
  The rounded cheeks which charm,
The grace of a buzzing circle,
  I saw but the wild alarm
Of the mazy, crazy habitant,
  And the long and bony arm.

And the house rose pale and stately
  Whose sentry was the moon ;
And the wind that crept around it
  Though howling, was a boon,
For compared to the screamings heard there
  To a storm, it was a swoon.

Along through the sounding entries
  I quickly made my way,
For the sound I heard so drearly
  Made me afraid to stay ;
Until on the topmost story
  I heard a meek voice say,

" O, lover, lover Everard Gray !
  Lover so true to me,

When will you come dear Everard Gray?
  Lover so good to me,
Oh, lover, lover Everard Gray,
  When will you come to me?

I followed the voice so closely,
  In the darkness of the night,
That I found the cell in a minute,
  With a panel to the right,
Which was closed with a spring — I opened,
  Revealing a pitiful sight.

The ray of the streaming moonlight,
  Glittered in fearlessly,
Lighting the cell — for it was one,
  So I could easily see.
But hark to the solemn chantings
  That came from the cell to me.

" Oh, lover, lover Everard Gray,
  Lover so true to me,
When will you come sweet Everard Gray?
  Lover so good to me.
Oh, lover, lover Everard Gray,
  When will you come to me?

A pallet of heavy timbers
  Was screwed against the wall,
And from the sides were pendant
  The chains on the limbs so small,

A mattrass of cornhusks covered
  Chairs and timbers and all.

But the voice and the words? ah! truly,
  How should I so forget
The sighings and throbbings of anguish,
  The wails of mild regret,
Of the lady chained to the pallet
  With eye and hair of jet?

Ah!pale and wofully saddened,
  Sat in that gloomy place,
One looking as if she were born to
  Every womanly grace, —
Sat passing intently up and down
  Her hand upon her face.

What can she mean? and the panel
  To open still more I dare,
For something moved me to ponder
  The cause of the downcast air,
Of that lovely woman sitting
  With a look of keen despair.

And I gazed with an intense yearning;
  That singular wailing freak
Made me dizzy — my eyes grew moist,
  And my knees grew cold and weak;
For still she rubbed with a whitened hand
  A spot upon her cheek.

Again I looked across the cell,
  And through the iron bars,
And saw that night the heavens bright,
  And saw the glistening stars,
Yet faintly poured that misery forth
  Whose tone my spirit jars.

" O, lover, lover Everard Gray !
  Lover so true to me,
When will you come dear Everard Gray ?
  Lover so good to me,
O, lover, lover Everard Gray !
  When will you come to me ?

Then she looked on her pallid hands,
  And the deep blue winding veins,
And she looked with a languid eye
  On incarcerating chains ;
Just as the beams of the solemn moon
  Fell on her hands and chains.

" Oh God ! " she cried, and starting up
  To her full woman height,
She glared upon the bluish ray
  With horrible affright ;
" That moon again — Oh God ! oh God !
  Oh ! take away the light."

" Oh ! take away the vaprous light,
  That brought me to repining,

Its fangs upon my temples throb,
    The thing of lizard lining;
It crawls upon my dreams a-nights
    And chills me with its shining."

And faster and faster moved her hand
    Over her ashen face,
And wilder and wilder flashed her eye,
    Bluer grew the place,
Lovely and yet more lovely seemed
    Each sad, yet intense grace.

" That moon! that moon!" she deeply spake,
    " On such a night as this
He led me forth, and told me
    Of such enduring bliss ;
I little thought so many chills
    Were in one little kiss.

" A few slight clouds were moving then,
    Betokening a storm,
When in my tent a soldier, I,
    I saw his well-known form ;
Oh God! will never this little cheek,
    Will *never* this cheek grow warm ?

" The night was cold, a fearful dream
    My brain pressed heavily,
When starting from the racks it brought
    I saw my Everard o'er me,

And from his forehead bare and white
　The blood-drops trickled freely.

" He beckoned me to follow him,
　' He had found a home,' he said,
And ' ere the morning sun should rise,
　We two should meet and wed;'
But now I think how much he looked
　As though he then were dead.

" I left my tent and passed the guard,
　Nor aught felt of alarm,
For I was leaning proudly on
　My own dear Everard's arm ;
He would protect, he manly said,
　My little form from harm.

" The moon it shone so brightly then
　O'er that entangled wood,
I fairly hugged my Everard's arm,
　I thought e'en as I should,
That what the sky so smiled upon
　Could not be else than good.

" Ah ! now I do remember more ; —
　The woods were densely thronged
With spectres that to earthly forms
　Could never have belonged,
For when they hissed they seemed to be
　Four-eyed and double tongued.

" And scorpions hung from out the leaves
  Of all the mouldy trees ;
And wolfish howls and dying moans,·
  Was the only kind of breeze,
And now to think of these dire things
  My blood begins to freeze.

" I saw a grinning skeleton,
  Nailed to a tree of Pine ;
A liver-colored serpent too
  That gnawed decaying swine,
Which from their recking bosoms came,
  And nestled into mine.

" The owlets chattered in my ears,
  The bats flew in my face,
And snails upon my arms that night
  Did slimy pathways trace,
While maggots played upon my feet —
  Oh ! 'twas a horrid place.

" We passed a haunted house ten times,
  And swam a toad-stirred brook,
A jabbering chainèd ghost we saw,
  A heedless child o'ertook ;
Yet all the while my Everard dear
  Ne'er gave me one kind look.

" And on, and on it seemed for miles,
  By thorny paths o'ergrown,

These sights had strangely weakened me,
  My strength was nearly gone ;
Yet on we went by gibbets scared
  That creaked and swayed alone.

" The sky was murky overhead ;
  The earth was but a flood
Of festering, crawling reptiles,
  And slimy, poisoned mud ;
The moon was one dull, dingy flame,
  And all the stars were blood.

" The stones were full of pestilence ;
  And noisome vapors filled
The atmosphere ; all living things
  'Neath blear-eyed night were stilled ;
Until I half called up the thought
  That Everard too was killed.

" We hurried on, and then he spoke,
  In a kind of blood-thick tone,
' This is the strangest wedding, dear,
  That ever yet was known.' —
I stumbled over something — looked,
  My Everard was gone.

" ' Oh Everard come back,' " I cried,
  For I was struck with fear,
When from a form upon the ground
  A voice came low but clear,

' Oh Ellen! see your lover true,
    Your Everard is here.'

" I flew to him, forgetting all,—
    The other world and this ;
He threw his arms around my neck —
    Oh ! what a feverish bliss,
And planted on my yielding cheek
    This long but chilling kiss.

" And then I saw him ghastly pale,
    I knelt down by his side,
I kissed the blood from his quivering lip,
    Forgetting all my pride,
He uttered only once my name,
    And then, alas ! he died.

" The moon gave forth a fitful glow,
    A kind of sombre green,
That lighted just enough to show
    The misery of the scene ;
And Everard's head lay cold and stiff,
    My loving arms between.

" I hugged his lifeless form to mine,
    That soon so chilly grew,
I sadly laid him gently down
    For I grew chilly too ;
And then I called him many times,
    For what else could I do ?

" No voice there was to answer mine ;
   No human aid was near ;
No arm to help me bear him up ;
   No kind receiving bier ;
Naught but the shiv'ring winds came there
   To freeze each sorrowing tear.

" I cut a lock of his glossy hair,
   A button from his coat,
A letter from his bosom took
   That I myself once wrote ;
But all the while a demon clutch
   Was tight around my throat.

I gasped for breath, my starting eyes
   Bloodshot and big became ;
My heart seemed but a heaving mass
   Of agonizing flame ;
Yet all the while his whitened corse
   Lay stiff, and cold the same.

" A fearful thought possessed me then,
   To never flag nor tire
Until the bosoms of all men
   Were filled with torments dire ;
For where my brain so lately was,
   Was now a hellish fire.

" I pressed him once again to me
   And stole his portrait, — this,

I wept his white hand full of tears,
   And once again did kiss,
Then wildly ran into the wood
   With many a howl and hiss.   .

" Oh! what I suffered then let none
   Attempt to make me tell,
But it was like the torture which
   The doomed ones find in hell;
The torments which have angels stung
   For ages since they fell.

" The path along the lonesome wood
   Was dotted o'er with graves;
Until I came to other woods,
   All filled with dismal caves,
And near their steaming entrances
   Stood many winged slaves,

" With horrid humps upon their backs,
   And horns their eyes between,
And scales grew on their shining arms;
   Some eyes were red, some green;
And such great pairs of grinning jaws
   I'm sure were never seen.

" And great, long, crooked, jagged claws
   They had for finger nails;
Their hair stood out like giant fins
   Of furious battling whales;

And when they laughed they seemed to mock
  The wintry midnight gales.

" Past these.with many a hurried glance
  In terror flight I flew,
Until my dress grew heavy with
  The weight of falling dew,
And then one caught me, — in his cave
  My shuddering form he drew.

" He told me in a whisper that
  He was an Antiquary;
That he had many a skeleton
  Of fish and fowl and fairy ;
That oft he roamed in deserts dark
  And mammoth tombs and airy.

" I felt his hot breath on my face,
  I heard his putrid sigh, .
As telling me his wedding day
  At length was drawing nigh ;
That he and I together soon
  Would meet in marriage tie.

" I shuddered mightily, yet said
  A short day he might dream on,
And then I laughed right heartily,
  A joke it was to scream on,
For a curious couple we would be,
  Me crazed, and he a demon.

" He led me through an entry dark,
 He stronger was than I,
Though to remove his claws from off
 My arm I oft did try;
And only begged a resting place
 That I might go and die.

" ' No; No,' the monster said ; ' not yet,'
 In voice of thundering glee,
' You have forgot the words I spoke,
 That you must marry me ;
But here we have a museum
 Which you must in and see.

" A viper stuffed, of green and gold
 Hung on the blackened wall,
With an infant's head between its teeth,
 Which seemed for bread to call;
And the viper swung on the wall where it hung,
 Until it seemed to crawl.

" A skeleton of a lordly man,
 Whose teeth were painted red,
So truly by machinery moved
 You scarce could think him dead ;
His jaws they moved, his hands were clasped,
 As though his prayers he said.

" A woman disembowelled lay,
 The sight my heart-strings wrung,

It shook my nerveless, failing limbs
 And paralyzed my tongue ;
One monkey tore her bowels out,
 One gave them to her young.

" A mother o'er a rotten shroud,
 In which her baby slept,
Was kneeling stiff, and stark, and cold,
 And stone-hard tears she wept,
While vermin o'er her haggard limbs
 All eager coiled and crept.

" ' Here is a tooth,' " the demon said,
 ' I from a leopard drew,
Who fed upon an angel like
 As anything to you ;
And here a mummy, spider-stuffed,
 A serpent's liver too.

" ' There is a tear from lovely maid
 Who once a lover lost,
And there the withered heart of him
 Who in a love was crossed,
And there a worm from Nero's grave,
 A bone, too, tempest tossed.

" ' And here a forkéd lightning's bolt
 That killed an answering bride,
And there the lungs of an anchorite
 Who female charms denied,

And hanging there a poem from
  A gifted man belied.

" ' Just over there a swollen brain
  Fresh from the battle's heat,
And here a little cherub's eye,
  Whose mother murdered it,
And there the landlord's tongue, that turned.
  A widow in the street.

" ' And here's a thief — a bandit chief,
  That used to kill for play,
But here's the gem of all of them,
  And proud am I to say,
Here is a little leaden ball
  That killed one Everard Gray.'

" A moment stood I paralyzed,
  As though struck quickly dead,
Then seized a bone and fiercely bruised
  Him, till his temples bled ;
In both his eyes I thrust a thumb,
  Then turned, and shrieking fled.

" The sky was murky overhead,
  The earth was but a flood
Of festering, crawling reptiles,
  And slimy, poisoned mud,
The moon was one dull, dingy flame,
  And all the stars were blood.

" Still on I ran, pursued by things
    On evil deeds intent,
Until a something challenged me
    Whose eyes were on me bent,
But what it was I cannot tell,
    For life was nearly spent.

" And then they brought me here I know,
    Where gloomy thoughts enwreath,
And every night these moonbeams come
    With the story of his death ;
Where every night the blue moonlight
    Shortens my little breath.

" And then this kiss, that once I thought
    Would evil spirits charm,
Colder, colder, and colder grows,
    As though 'twould never be warm ;
Ah me ! — it fills my creeping soul
    With terrible alarm.

" What's that ?   Oh God ! the blessed sight —
    I wonder will he stay.
Comes he to say farewell to me,
    Or take me soon away ?
Nearer — ah! truly 'tis indeed —
    He comes, — my Everard Gray.

" O,   lover, lover Everard Gray,
    Lover so true to me !

Where did you get that winding sheet ?
Why weep you bitterly ?
  Come, put your arm around my neck,
And sit me on your knee."

Awhile she gazed, intently wrapped,
  Along the whitened wall,
Until her eyes were a looking out
  Of the barred windows and small ;
Her very soul seemed bound up in
  A Heaven-ensighted thrall.

" Don't leave me here, my Everard dear,
  Come back my Everard true ;
Don't leave me here, with spectres drear,
  Of green and white and blue.
Come back I say!" and she beat the bars
  Till blood from her fingers flew.

" Come back, come back, or a demon dark
  Shall bring you back, I say —
Ah! faithless monster ! cruel fiend !
  Ah, faithless Everard Gray ! "
And with a shrill and harrowing shriek,
  She leaped from the bars away.

Never a scene like that saw man,
  Never need wish to see,
As she flung herself against the wall
  With fearful energy,

Till the blood was gurgling from her mouth
    And curdling frightfully.

O'erwrought by tears and dreadful gloom,
    I left the fated cell,
And down the echoing stairways passed,
    To where the moonbeams fell
Upon the smoothly gravelled walks,
    That I had learned so well.

Next morn I sought the keeper out,
    And he shook his hoary head —
" This morn, stone dead, they picked her up
    In the court yard there," he said,
And he dropped a tear to the memory of
    The woman soldier dead.

.

THE BIG WHISKY PUNCH ;

OR, A NEW YANKEE DOODLE.

WASTE OF WHISKY, — At Martinsburg, Va., Gen. Williams
made what the boys called a monster toddy by knocking out the
heads of two hundred and fifty barrels of new "old rye," *alias*
corn whisky, at the still owned by Lieutenant Col. Stuart, of
the Confederate forces, and pouring most of it into the neighbor-
ing brook. A guard was at first put over it to protect it, but the
smell of the whisky was so strong that it overpowered them and
they slept on their posts. Then came the thirsty ones, and their
name was legion, and drank of the liquor with evil consequences
to themselves and the public. Hence the General's great toddy
making.— *Phil. Evening Bulletin.*

At Martinsburg, one Stuart owned
  A " Still," I think they call it,
And as it was a quaint affair
  I'll tell what did befal it.
This Stuart when he left the place,
  ' He left so fast and frisky,
That he forgot to take his " still " ·
  And many pipes of whisky.
      CHORUS —Yankee Doodle Martinsburg,
              Yankee Doodle Whisky,
              Yankee Doodle, Williams made
              A punch so fast and frisky.

This Still it stood upon the bank,
  Perhaps just where it "oughter"
As Stuart said " that it was so
  Convenient to the water."
Not that he liked the latter drink,
  It never made him frisky,
But simply for the use it was
  Of thinning out his whisky.

When General Williams reached the town,
  There was no need to " shell it,"
For young and old were jolly drunk,
  His own men 'gan to smell it.
But Williams fearing that his boys
  Might too get drunk and frisky,
Straight said " the water should be made
  Like half-and-half with whisky."

" Oh General, surely that's a joke,
  You really did not taste it,
For if you did you'd not incline
  So savagely to waste it ! "
" But soldiers, you know men are men,
  And war is rather risky,
So you had better pour it out —
  The glorious old rye whisky."

And so as they were ordered, soon,
  They 'gan to knock the heads in,
        2*

While some who stopped to take a drink
  Soon went and got their beds in.
For aye it was a jolly brand, —
  For jollities so frisky,
And Williams' sober thought we praise,
  For pouring out the whisky.

And soon the creek began to smell,
  So very strong and mighty,
The very birds upon the trees
  Felt unusually flighty.
The cows drew near and took a sniff,
  And 'gan to sport so frisky,
And I believe they made that day,
  A milk-punch with the whisky.

A rustic happening along
  Just thought he'd stop a minute,
To find whence came the funny smell,
  Exclaimed " the deuce is in it."
" Behanged I think these pretty times,
  And drinking rather risky,
For what I thought was water pure,
  Has turned to right good whisky."

Two constables then came that way
  And saw the rustic sip, sirs,
So they took out their nippers so,
  And thought they'd " take a nip sirs."

And so they drank and soon got drunk,
  Upon the bank side frisky,
Each wanted to arrest himself,
  For stealing old rye whisky.

A brewer stout of hops, hops by,
  Who fills the eye of madam's,
He takes a drink and vows that this
  Is better ale than " Adam's,"
He joins the other three and now,
  They have a dance so frisky,
The police bruise the brewer, and
  The rustic sticks to whisky.

At last so thick the stream became,
  By whisky in it sunk,sirs,
That General Williams had to cry,
  " Hold or I shall be drunk,sirs !
By Jove! I thought I had the nerve
  To stand it, but its risky,
So place a guard about the rest
  Of that teasing old rye whisky.

The guard was placed but sad to tell,
  Yet we can reason through it,
The smell of whisky made them sleep,
  But hardships could not do it.
And Williams said, when told of this,
  " I knew t'was much too risky,

So I must e'en forgive the men
   For sleeping on the whisky.

An idea struck a happy man
   In faith t'was very well sirs,
To throw a load of lemons in
   To take away the smell sirs.
The Soldiers all alive became,
   And went to work quite brisky,
For anything was better than
   The strong smell of raw whisky.

Just now a rebel line of teams
   Appeared with horses goaded,
Which happened to turn out to be
   With Orleans sugar loaded.
So they were seized and Williams now,
   Appeared so gay and frisky,
" Put in the sugar, boys, ha, ha!
   We'll have a punch of whisky."

Just then news came, and Williams said,
   " Be ready, boys, instanter,
The enemy are just ahead,"—
   He set off on a canter.
And you all know what then he did
   Instead of getting frisky,
And if you don't — no matter 'tis,
   I only sing of whisky.

TO A FOUNDLING. *

An Old Trick.— About 9 o'clock last night an infant was placed in the arms of a negro woman at Broad and Market streets, and she was requested to hold it for a while. The colored lady waited with the child for about half an hour, but the lady came not to recover her infant. The infant was taken in charge by a neighbor, who named it BUTLER McCLELLAN. — *Phil. Inquirer.*

Little babe! little babe!
Little babe, say;
Why do you slumber here?
Tell me I pray.
Why on this sunny day
Comest thou here,
With no one to wipe away
Each little tear?
No one to chuckle thee
Under the chin,
No one to tickle thee
Making a din,
None to caress thee
Shield from the storm,
None to hard press thee
On a breast warm,
Little babe, why?

* Supposed to be addressed to Butler McClellan by the lady who took him in charge.

Where was thy Mother's heart?
  Little babe, say,
She played no mother's part
  Thee to betray.
Was she a woman, babe?
  Did she have eyes?
Did she look human, babe,
  Whom thee could despise?
Dwelt she in city?
  Lived she forlorn?
Deserving of pity,
  Or meriting scorn?
      Which of them, babe?

Danced thou in the sunlight
  Into this world?
Or in the dark midnight
  Was't suddenly hurl'd?
Was music then playing
  Its gladsomest tones?
Or was there one praying
  For new little ones?
Or was there sweet singing?
  Or was there a curse?
Was there a brawl bringing
  Anything worse?
      Little babe, which?

Come, be thou near me,
  This bosom will greet,

Nay do not fear me
  Little babe sweet.
Come babe and tell me
  All thy life through
If griefs ere befel thee?
  What things thou can'st do?
Can'st walk a wee-bit?
  Or sing like a bird?
Play with " Carlo " or " Kit "?
  Or lisp out a word?
      Can'st thou, dear babe?

See from the tree yonder
  A leaf drops away,
And a little girl fonder
  Of leaves than of play,
Takes it up rovingly,
  Gives it a look,
Places it lovingly
  Into her book.
Thy mother 's that tree,
  Dear little elf!
The leaf it is thee,
  The girl is myself,
The Book is my home.
  Smallest of men!
Dearest babe! come
  Laugh out again.
Little babe once!
  Now once again!

THE SOLDIER OF THE THIRD.

Among those who fell was one old man whose head was white with age, and whose story is a romance of war. He had been thirty years in the regular service as a private soldier. He had followed the Indians through the everglades of Flori la, bivouack-ed upon the side of the Rocky Mountains, chased the Camanche and the Cherokee through New Mexico, stood before the fire of Buena Vista, charged up the heights of Chepultepec, and followed the victorious flag of his country along the plaza of Mexico and into the halls of the Montezumas. His arms was covered with cheverons, six blue stripes indicating six consecutive enlistments, and two red battle-stripes, typifying Florida and Mexico ; and with these simple insignia he felt prouder than ever did the white-plumed Murat at the head of his gaudy cavalry. He fell in the heat of battle, with the shouts of his comrades ringing in his ears. Poor fellow ! Lowly among the brave, almost forgotten in this age of ingratitude and forgetfulness, who shall relate his eventful and glorious history ?—*Phil. Press.*

The war din at Manassas rolled back to yonder
    sky
The thunders of the day before, to pall the tem-
    pest's cry,
And Justice who but lately was chanting peaceful
    hymns,
Hurled down fierce notes of rage at the serpent
    round her limbs,
There Right had raised his steady arm, and glared
    his eagle eye,

To crush the traitrous mass who seemed to woo the
    battle's ply,
The bounding bombs usurped the plowman's busy
    word,
Presaging wakeful glory, to the strong and gallant
    " Third."

In that band of rushing warriors beat hearts in
    rivalry,
Who should do most to aid the cause of sacred
    liberty,
Is it lose an arm, a leg or eye, or fall with shatter-
    ed heart,
To prove who loves their country most, must with
    that country part?
But with a wilder throb and a lighter step I ween,
Is yon hoary-headed soldier with the lofty colors
    seen,
And e'er the trumpet sounds to move, his patriot
    voice is heard,
Be ready all ye soldiers, ye gallants of the " Third."

The charge is made — he madly shouts, his heart
    now feels no pause,
Its blood is all on tiptoe for the triumph of his
    cause.
Now hand to hand engaging, now at the cannon's
    mouth,
Now cutting down a gunner, some minion of the
    South.

But see ! he falters, bear him up ye sinewey arms
    and strong !
He's old and weak and cannot stand the fiery on-
    set long.
Alas ! a ball has hit him, for now a shriek is heard,
And the hand is growing cold that bore the colors
    of the " Third."

Two comrades caught him as he fell, and to the
    side they bore
The yielding form now stifled with the weight of
    clotted gore,
That gathered in his throat and choked his utter-
    ance down,
For the wound was in his breast, be it said to his
    renown ;
But the first sharp sickening shock of the fatal
    ball's career.
Is ended as he lifts his head and begs his comrade's
    ear,
"How goes the battle, soldiers," in a faint dim
    voice is heard
" Do the colors still float proudly o'er the gallants
    of the " Third ? "

" Aye, aye old man, bear up awhile, nor let thy
    old heart fret,
For God is with the Right,   Victory shall be with
    us yet,

Soothe the surgings of thy eagle heart, and curb
    thy restless mind,
Lie thee still awhile, right speedily the surgeon we
    will find."
" Comrade, comrade, stay! I'm death-hit, this is
    cureless agony.
Stay by my side and strain your eyes, and tell me
    what you see,
For I want to hear before I die what I have always
    heard,
The victor cheers of triumph, from the strong and
    mighty " Third."

With eyes now fixed in deadly pain, he sat and
    watched the strife,
He'd given up for what he loved, his gray but
    cheerful life,
And now though each convulsive throb, with agony
    shook his frame,
And each dry and panting heart-beat, was a ghast
    and quivering flame,
He struggled nobly to endure, that he might yet
    enjoy,
And wept because a manly strength, he might ne'er
    again employ.
With mingled shame and anguish in his feeble bo-
    som stirred,
He is growing faint and listless, the soldier of the
    " Third."

The waving of the foliage above his dying place,
Caused a stirring of the eye-lids, and a glowing of
    the face,
For memories of other wars retinge his cheeks with
    red,
Where full of life beneath the trees he leaped nor
    felt a dread.
How when but twelve as drummer boy, against a
    foreign foe
At Lundy's Lane, he boldly to the battle field did
    go.
His father was the only kin, whose voice he'd ever
    heard,
His father was the army — the bold and dauntless
    " Third."

Now thick and fast came memories of many a bat-
    tle plain,
They brighten up his eye, and fire up his brain,
When seeking out the Indian, a callous, wily foe,
All through the swamps of Florida, he fearlessly
    did go,
On the mountains of the West, on the plains of
    Mexico
Victory always on his standard, would a righteous
    cause bestow,
And now to cheat him of his fame, no envious
    tone is heard,
For stiff and stark is growing cold the soldier of
    the "Third."

His comrades lay him gently down, and with a
 heavy sigh
They leave him, grasp their muskets, and to the
 battle hie.
' Twas very sweet to think that this old man of
 chivalry,
Should breathe his latest breath in the arms of
 memory.
Here's a dipping of a pen to his deeds that glow
 amain !
Here's a sighing of the heart, for each deep throb
 of pain !
Here's a soul-gift from the eye, which is falling
 though unheard,
Perchance may speak my sorrow for the soldier of
 the " Third."

TO EDMUND RUFFIN:

THE VENERABLE MAN WHO FIRED THE FIRST GUN AT FORT SUMPTER.

Gray though thy hairs be; though deep penetra-
    tion
  Sits in those eyes which once liberty loved,
Yet gladly thou look'st on thy land's desecration,
  And false to her flag hast dastardly proved.

Oh! where was the blood that had sacredly borne
    thee,
  That mantled with pride thy fond mother's face?
Did it not rise in blackness and fire to scorn thee,
  And scorch the foul thought that stains her fair
    race?

Oh! where were the hands that to fame would
    have led thee,
  From danger and woe were put forth to save?
Were they not clasped in sorrow, that truth had
    so fled thee
  As palsied, thy father rose from his wronged
    grave?

Tho' at present thou art all befondled and flattered,
   Yet know that a bitter day has yet to come ;
The time will yet be when thy bones will be
     scattered,
   And none will be found to gather them home.

Thy name and thy state — the first at our na-
     tion
   That ever an aged man willingly aimed, —
Will single thee out from this whole generation
   As one to be loathed e'en when traitors are
     named.

Youth and hot blood, may be some palliation,
   For crimes that are wrought 'gainst pretended
     wrongs ;
But Ruffin ! *thy wrinkles* cry out " accusation,
   And guilt threescore fold to thy fame now be-
     longs.

Though the days that are left thee be moments of
     quiet,
   Yet think of the grave that must soon yawn
     before,
And think of the time when those who'll pass by it
   Will cast the hot spurn at the stone standing
     o'er.

OUR RIFLE AND BAYONET.

In the moonlight gleaming
   On the edge of thicket,
Keeping off the dreaming
   From a drowsy picket,
All alive with listening
   If a noise is heard,
All alive with glistening,
   Instinctive as a bird.

Proud and stately flashing
   In the morning sun,
Through the rebels crashing
   Till the battle's won ;
Over mountains pressing,
   Fearless on the crag,
Every storm caressing,
   Like our gallant flag.

Eager to be bursting
   On the upstart foe,
Marching without thirsting,
   Day and night 'twill go.

Now a foe lies bleeding
　'Neath its reeking blade,
Almost nerveless, pleading,
　While a prayer is made.

Swung aloft all reeking
　In the bloody strife,
Each new moment seeking
　Out another life.
In the valley lying
　From the thundering strife,
Says a rustic, spying,
　. "Here's a jolly knife."

Down a chimney going,
　Makes an M. D. dance,
Picks it up so knowing,
　Thinks it is a lance.
Cobblers hit while waxing
　An eternal end,
Thinks the awl is taxing
　What the law won't mend.

On the ship appearing,
　Sailor speaks a wish,
That no harm is nearing
　From that curious fish.
In the schoolroom hinting
　To the boys who nod,

Who quickly take to squinting
   At master's tickling rod.

Sewing woman, dreaming,
   Heavily doth sigh,
Because this needle seeming-
   ly hath got no eye.
Southern swells are moaning,
   And are growing sick,
Don't like Yankee honing,
   Nor the Scott tooth-pick.

All their army paling,
   (Our fencing does'nt please),
At prospect of the railing
   They will get from these.
They've many things been stealing
   From Uncle's pocket large,
No sign of thanks revealing,
   The record is, " to charge."

Let them beware the raking
   When gathered are our men ;
They won't admire the making
   Of charges with this pen.
Logically we're going
   Their vitals to anoint,
By critically showing
   Them *so* fine a point,

Adepts in art of *rifling*,
  Light fingers and dark eyes,
We'll show them there's no trifling
  In our *Sharpe* replies.

When they see *our* rifling
  Thick and fast and sore,
They will say, all stifling,
  " What a horrid bore! "
Funny, though no funning,
  Arms all thrown away,
To see the *body* running
  Off their legs away.

Proud and stately flashing
  In the morning sun,
Through the rebels crashing,
  Till the battle's won.
Over mountains pressing,
  Fearless on the crag,
Every storm caressing
  Like our gallant flag.

PHILIP'S VICTORY OVER PHILLIS.

Philip and Phillis a once loving pair,
  Of late very quarrelsome grew ;
She said it was foul, he said it was fair,
  He vowed it was black and she blue.
So after a day of perpetual strife,
  With oaths full many a score,
He said " he would make an end of this life,
  By going down South to the War."

" Oh Philip my dear, do you mean what you say ? "
  In a tone of sarcasm and fire,
Sweet Phillis replied — " Oh hurry I pray,
  'Tis just the thing I desire.
And if while under the orders you tread
  Of McClellan or General Banks,
A stray cannon ball shall take off your head,
  Pray give it my very best thanks."

"All right, my loving and womanly dear,
  Of charity the example,
If that occurs I'll often be here
  On your brain and breast to trample.

Such horrid visions your brain shall bear,
   On your breast such demons shall tread,
That you'll start from out a vicious nightmare
   To see my ghost by your bed."

" But remember my dear, my Phillis dear,
   Things may not take place as you've willed,
And though I'd rather be dead than here,
   Perchance I shall *not* be killed ;
And then you shall see me stalking in,
   With golden epaulets bright,
And in a thundering voice begin
   To rack your soul with affright."

" No matter, I care not, let come what will,
   No need of a futher scoff,
I care not, you see, that the wars should kill,
   If they only *take you off.*
Suppose you come back with your epaulets bright,
   And your thundering voice's doom.
You've oft called me witch, I'll turn one outright,
   And flee to the clouds on a broom."

" But Phillis my dear, perhaps you have heard
   In parlor or kitchen or hall.
Of a thing that at three miles brings down a bird,
   In the shape of an Armstrong ball,
And then to think of the awful mishap
   Of being brought down *with a stick,*

Of giving your head a death dealing rap,
  On the edge of a simple brick.

" Perhaps when lying all cold and flat
  You will own I truly have said,
It is better to have a brick in your hat
  Than to have it in your head.
But no more, I am done, my curse I bequeath,
  And by the beautiful stars,
By the heavens above, by the place beneath,
  I'm off to the merciful wars.

" Good bye sweet Phillis " — a kiss he dared
  To steal, spite the frowns she wore ;
And picking up a bundle prepared,
  He darted through the door.
But the wilful voice of Phillis so sweet,
  And which she had cause to deplore,
Said " Good bye, of all things never retreat,
  And, oh pray, come back no more."

Now Philip so weary had grown of late
  Of this domestic strife,
That a little plan had entered his pate
  To reform his still dear wife.
So in a soldiers suit he arrayed
  His form, a mustache he wore,
Determined at night he would serenade
  His Phillis, before her door.

Night came, and with a guitar in hand
    He briskly wended his way,
Through the tangled brush, and some o'ergrown
       land,
    And thinking what he should play.
At last he arrived at his cottage white
    Which life or death to him brings,
And the moon was shining never so bright,
    As he touched his hand to the strings.

And after playing a plaintive strain
    That seemed like a melting prayer,
He sang " Sweet be thy Rest," not in vain,
    For a window opens there.
And Phillis all decked in night-cap white
    Pretending a sleepy stare,
Slowly asked " what means this outcry at night?
    Who the devil is it there?"

So he sang " loved wife of this bosom true,
    Oh hear my wail I beg,"
But she, the loved wife, seized upon and threw
    At Phil. a rotten egg.
Who, finding this attempt had failed,
    With passion bubbled o'er,
He soon resolved, and straight assailed
    The fastenings on his door.

She barricades, he threatens mightily,
    And swears, believing it no sin,

Until down goes the door, and frightfully,
  He boldly rushes in.
And Phillis trembles now amain
  Phil. draws a bowie knife,
She vows she ne'er will fight again,
  He swears he'll take her life.

Phil. said " the soldiers' orders were,
  As dear to them as life,
My Colonel made each soldier swear
  That each would kill his wife.
Now I have been a husband long,
  A loving one and true,
Your time has come, 'tis not *my* wrong,
  I'm *ordered* to kill you."

" But Phillis, my orders were this night,
  At which I did not repine,
To usher you to a *heaven of light*,
  With a strain of music divine.
Perhaps I might have saved your life—
  At least for it I could beg,
But pity flew, and out flew my knife,
  When you threw that rotten egg.

" Prepare, prepare " and the room grew dense
  With a bluish kind of air,
And the fiends caught up the awful sense
  Of the hellish word, " Prepare."

" Forgive, forgive ! " and the trembling voice
   Begged that it yet might live,
And the room responds, the spirits rejoice, —
   At the words " forgive, forgive."

" Wilt ever be humble and gentle and meek,
   Submissive and tender and true,
Oh woman ! remember to whom you speak,
   For *I* am speaking to you."
Phil. said in a tone of thundering might,
   As if rage was bursting his heart,
And he listened while in a tone of affright,
   His wife this vow did impart : —

" Oh, husband, I never will speak a word,
   Which may thy soul displease,
And if ever in Heaven a prayer was heard
   May mine be ; — here on my knees
I'll ask that God, I've offended so oft,
   That both he and thou wilt forgive."
And Phillis all meek held her hands aloft
   And murmured, " Forgive and let live ! "

" Philis rise, and come to my bosom, wife ! "
   Phil.'s tears did well nigh choke,
" It was only to cure that wicked strife
   Of yours that I coined this *joke*."
" Oh husband you've conquered just as you should
   A peace ere it was too late.
I promise to ever continue a good,
   A peaceful and loving mate."

A CHORUS FROM THE CREW OF THE "PETREL."

SUNG TO A TUNE EXTEMPORISED.

Merrily jingled the bells all then,
    Jingled the bells all merrily,
When out of Charleston harbor sailed
    We of the " Petrel," *We.*
The sun had never so brightly shone,
    Never so brightly shone he,
As filling our rag and waving our flag,
    We stoutly put to sea.

Joyfully bubbled the waves all then,
    Bubbled the waves so joyfully,
That " Uncle Sam " was quite forgot
    By those in the " Petrel," *We.*
And the stately ship that hove in sight
    We thought to easily flee,
But she showed us her guns, from a myriad
      of suns,
    She blowed us into the sea.

Mournfully jingle the bells all now,
    Jingle the bells all mournfully ;

And from " Moyamensing's " windows look
   We of the " Petrel," *We.*
Perhaps a scaffold will be our end,
   Oh men, ye all will agree,
There's but little fun, and naught to be won,
   In pirating on the sea.

SONNET ON WAR.

Thou minister of vengeful passion, War!
   Thou devastating lightning's seething flood!
   We hail thee as the master god of blood,
The gloss of sin, of death the other star.
When first on sunny earth, thy curse appeared,
   Mankind was fixed to peaceful, kindly arts
   That rolled content upon their thankful hearts,
While on a pearl-couch cherub Love was reared.
But now all changed to melancholic throbs
   An unassuaged wrath of tireless strength
   Heaves up our land's entire breadth and length,
And Love is crushed by fratricidal mobs
Oh, engine of the fiends! destruction's sign!
Life's most tumultuous heavy, griefs are thine.

LINES TO ONE WHO HAD A BROTHER IN THE REBEL ARMY.

(BOTH BEING FRIENDS OF THE AUTHOR.)

Thy brother in the rebel cause,
　Which many States have wrecked,
Now bids defiance to the laws
　Which those States did protect.
No task indeed, be thine to send
　Reproach or idle word,
He might himself with those defend
　While hate his bosom stirred.
But rather let some afterthought
　In sorrow wreathe his heart,
That kindred lives so dearly bought,
　He should attempt to part.

Why does his once true soul now spurn
　The flag he used to cheer,
And hail with sentiments that burn
　Like the applauding tear?
Those honored heroes of the past,
　Whose memories float high

As lightning banner of the blast,
　Or eagles in the sky ;
Why should he so forget *their* names ?
　Is he beyond the reach
Of those whose influence steady flames
　With lessons which they teach ?

Misled is he by fawning men —
　Could time such change impart ?
In youth ne'er false — he now, as then,
　Shuns treason in his heart.
Though victory's cup full oft we drink,
　Though failure lights upon
His standard, yet I proudly think
　Both hearts still beat as one ;
And though cut off from early scenes
　Oh ! think these times the veil,
Which 'twixt the skylight intervenes
　To droughted lands assail ;
The grass springs fresh, the lily's cup
　Beneath it's touch revives ;
The clouds move off, earth brightens up,
　Again affection lives.

Let winged destruction hurl its woe
　Across our lovely land,
Until all panting 'neath each throe,
　Our homes embrace the sand.
What though the black domestic fiend
　Should ride upon our necks,

And drape the hopes on which we leaned,
    With blood and human wrecks ?
What though the rebel's murderous though
    The civil broil instil ?
Oh, care not that *their* fame he's sought,
    He is thy brother still !

QUERIES (?)

Our Willie in the arbor sat,
    And eat the grapes all day
So fast, that very soon I thought
    That he would *fall away.*
Said I to Amy " can'st thou tell
    Why Will, the drunkard's road
Usurps ? and why his being drunk
    Makes him a cannon's load ? "
My Amy straightway gave it up —
    To guess was not her lot ;
So I exclaimed — " you see it is,
    Because he is *Grape Shot.*"
Amy smiled faintly, 'twas like no laugh at all,
Saying " 'tis plain *your wits are at a ball.*"

THE LADY OF THE LIEUTENANT COLONEL.

A lady fair to look upon
  In a darkened chamber lay,
And though 'twas only afternoon
  (So the mantel clock did say,)
But little light came into the room
  From the flush of outside day.

Motionless lay the lady fair,
  A picture of wondrous grace,
With a hand so small and an arm so white,
  That the Earth seemed not her place ;
But grief with ruthless hand had clutched
  The roses from her face.

Just now she stirred — a tear-drop fell
  From her holy lighted eye,
And over the face of a portrait ran
  As she uttered low a cry,
That from her soul in sadness wrought
  A kind of murmuring sigh.

" 'Three months agone, and a joyous wife
     I sat upon his knee,
And marked the starting place of the smiles
     That he used to smile to me,
But ah! that face and its welcoming smile
     I never more shall see.

" Three months agone — ere the chilling note
     Of the trumpet of war was heard,
I leapt, and danced, and laughed, and sang
     Light-hearted as a bird.
But a gloomy three months time has passed
     Since warmth this bosom stirred.

" And then the day, the horrible day,
     When a demon came from beneath,
With a wicked tale of his being shot,
     To take away my breath ;
Ah me! the news of that battle field
     Has well nigh caused my death.

" Yon clock, that stands on the mantel there
     Whose music he loved, he said,
Marked when our rapture rose with the sun
     But never with it fled,
Must be removed, for its mournful ring,
     Seems like the voice of the dead.

" Ah ! never a kinder heart than his
     Was part of man's estate,

Friendship had never to ask but once, —
   The poor had never to wait,
With his generous gift a prince he made
   Of the beggar at his gate.

" Could not a less manlier form be found
   To lead in the battle's ply?
For never a nobler soul had man,
   Never so searching an eye,
Never a love but his could so
   Thrill woman with a sigh.

" Each movement of the curtain,
   A solemn cadence is,
The ticking of the watch I wear,
   Puts me in mind of his.
Dead — dead — ah! would my head were laid
   Upon the field with his.

" There's our boy upon the doorstep —
   The almost infant reveller,
Tossing about unconsciously,
   I hear his ringing laughter,
And though I love to hear him so
   Each trill is a reminder.

" For it warns me of the times agone
   When near me one would hover,
And tell me of adventures
   He met with as a rover.

Ah me ! so bitterly of the time
   When my husband was a lover.

" Suppose his spirit should visit me,
   Should in yon chair appear,
Methinks I could look on the dead all night
   And never feel a fear,
Though he were pale and bleeding, I'd be
   So happy were he here.

" But that ringing at the door-bell !
   How my heart begins to swim,
At this moment too, is't possible ?
   My eyes are growing dim,
By the beating of this bosom
   It must be news of him."

Quickly comes the little footsteps
   Gently pattering like rain,
" Soul be silent for the message —
   Comes the boy to ease my pain ?
Bursts he in with joy exclaiming
   ' Papa has come home again.'

" Papa home, you little cherub
   Do you know what you have said,
Papa dearest, never can come home
   You know, boy, he is dead,
And far up with the angels, pet,
   He sleeps — the blameless dead."

" I know better, for I saw him
    And mamma, I tried to hide ;
But he kissed me, asked to see you,
    And his coat was blue and wide,
In his hat was father's feather,
    And his bright sword at his side."

" Papa home ! thou dearest treasure,
    Kiss me that again he's home,
Closer boy ! run now and tell him,
    Run and tell him I will come,
Run and hug, and kiss, and bless him,
    And kiss him till I come.

" But this dress so sombre would pall him,
    And place on his joy a bar,
It must off, for I feel so plainly
    These weeds a libel are,
With my soul and body in mourning
    To laugh I would not dare.

" What shall I wear ? the poplin gown
    Which so did please him then,
My bridal dress more fitting is
    Than my poplin gown of green ;
'Twas in that dress I took him first,
    It shall receive again.

" Throw open full wide the shutters,
    Oh ! that breeze it comes to me,

As 'twere the liberating breath
  That sets my spirit free,
Through the former gloom of the curtain
  The bright blue heavens I see.

" Ring out thou clock on the mantel !
  What time is it now ? just four —
'Twas just the same hour he left me
  To go to the terrible war,
But now his dangers appalling
  Like all my sorrows, are o'er.

"Again shall I leap with the merriment
  Of the joyous days agone,
Again shall my generous laughter
  Give the lie to a chilling moan,
Again shall I laugh with the loving zest
  For I will not be alone.

" I wonder if I am much changed, —
  For sixteen I used to pass,
Let me see ! how the cheeks are faded
  And sunken the eyes, alas !
I have grown, too, somewhat thinner,
  For I see it in the glass.

" There, now the dress is upon me,
  How fits it Betty, my dear ?
It seems to hang very loosely,
  About my form just here,

Ah ! my form is thinner and longer,
   Else why is it looser here ?

" But my voice, Betty dear, oh, tell me —
   (Prythee my 'kerchief bring)
Does it still preserve its freshness
   The strong and joyous ring
As of old, when those love-lipped ballads
   He used to hear me sing ?

" Will never this cheek grow florid ?
   Never glow bright this eye ?
Never this hair flow in ringlets ?
   Ne'er leave my bosom the sigh ?
Will never these arms be strong again
   To bring his bosom nigh ?

" Seems yet a dread o'er me creeping,
   To palsy me even here,
Seems over the joys I am feeling
   To run a chillsome fear,
On the sky-capped hopes I'm weaving
   There seems to hang a tear.

" Betty, dear, am I almost ready ?
   Pray tell me how I look.
Do I look like one who but lately
   Seemed of the world forsook ?
Very well, indeed ! then pray hand me,
   Yon golden clasped book.

" Betty, thank you — this book the ' Leaflets
  Of Memory ' he gave to me
'Twas just as the golden sunset
  Touched the tops of each waving tree —
And here is the rich dedication
  In his own dear hand, you see.

" Is each fold of the dress becoming ?
  Each ribbon in its place ?
Each bracelet and pin well suited?
  Does wave each ringlet with grace ?
Is my step both hearty and lightsome ?
  Does a smile enwreath my face ?

" Ah, tell me, Betty, I pray you !
  'Twould be a horrible sin,
To go down to him all untidy,
  With my voice a screeching din,
With a step so lagged and loathsome,
  And my smile a ghastly grin.

"All ready, I thank you, my Betty.
  Pray watch my faltering feet,
For already with wild excitement
  My heart begins to beat,
And I know not if I can safely
  Trust my brain and its whirlsome heat.

" Stay with me until you see him
  Beckon me to his arms,

Which ever more shall enclose me
  From the dreadful war's alarms.
Watch me closely till you see me
  Safe enfolded in his arms.

" Good bye, to the solemn cadence
  Of the dimly lighted room,
Good bye, to the solemn tickings
  So very suggestive of gloom ;
I go to the husband and lover,
  I go to a new life's bloom.

" Quickly comes the little footsteps
  Gently pattering like rain,
Bless the boy, he's quelled the throbbings
  Of this anxious bosom's pain.
Kiss me, boy ! — Where is your father ?
  Let me see his face again.

" Mother, this way, in the parlor
  Father is awaiting you,
Steady, mother, dearest mother,
  These tremblings shake you through.
Ah, mother 'twill be joyful,
  The meeting of you two ! "

" Run and tell him, boy, I'm coming,
  Then my smile thou may'st win.
Run and tell, and hug, and bless him,
  Dearest boy, thy task begin."

" Mother sweet, I pray you let me,
   Mother let me take you in."

" Well boy as thou wishest, be it,
   Open wide the parlor door.
Betty, for the world don't let me,
   Sink upon the surging floor."
" Mother there he is — Oh, see him
   Father — mother 's at the door."

" Boy thou liest ! It is not he,
   Let me look — oh, look again,
Though he has a noble bearing,
   For this deed, the brand of Cain
Be upon him — no, not that bad,
   Though he's split my heart in twain."

" I am a Captain, madam,
   Of your noble husband's corps.
I came to bring you sad news,
   Your husband is no more.
I came to bring this loyal blade,
   The sword your husband wore.

" The foeman of our much loved land
   Had need to wear a shield,
Who e'er our Colonel brave did strike
   Lay cold upon the field,—
A victim to the righteous wrath
   In which his arm was steeled.

" But, madam, nations need a spur,—
    A martyr's eloquence,
To rouse them from the seeds of sloth,
    To deeds of eminence.
For such an one our leader took
    His life, and bore it hence.

" A nation, madam, mourns with you,
    A nation bleeds to-day,
That woes like ours must needs bear
    The talented away.
The nation weeps, while thanking you
    For him, lost in the fray."

"Come closer, boy — aye, closer still,
    Support me, Betty, dear,
Good day, sir! who would think, my boy
    I had so large a tear —
When lately I've so many shed,
    From sorrow's fountain, here.

Ah! well I knew the joyful news,
    Was but a well coined lie,
That spread it's venom o'er my frame,
    The tears of love to dry.
That I should live to see this day —
    Quick, water, or I die!"

In Betty's arms the lady fair,
    While Betty softly prayed,
4

So white, and, ah, so motionless
  Was all serenely laid,
Until more help came, then her form
  Was to the bed conveye

That night upon her couch she lay,
  And tossed each weary limb,
As though in dreams she spectres met,
  So gaunt, and gray, and grim,
And 'twas many days ere she could think
  Or talk of aught save him.

THE LOVE OF THE WOUNDED ZOUAVE.

A Zouave lay in a sorry plight,
  In the hospitual, weary and sore,
And in faith it was a right sorry sight
  To see the wounds that he bore.

A bandage of white was round the head
  Of this Union man and true,
But his nose and his trowsers were very red
  And his spirit and eyes were blue.

Now three days' suns had risen and set
  Since first on that bed he lay;
His fever was gone — no more he would fret,
  When the nurses passed that way.

Around him men of many a mould
  Lay proud of the wounds they bore,
Whose hearts were wreathed in a purpose bold
  And whose faces were wreathed with gore.

His shoulder no more the knapsack held,
  His arm had no musket there,

And though his head was very much swelled,
  It had very little hair.

The sweets of tobacco could do no harm,
  So he their presence invoked ;
Though he had " regalia " on his arm,
  He another grimly smoked.

And so we see him at leisure now,
  In comparative quiet and ease,
But look at the stern though upraised brow
  As a gliding form he sees.

The rosy cheeks' fresh glow of health,
  The bright eye's lovely hues,
Pictured to him a mine of wealth,
  " But ah ! should she refuse ?

" What should she be of high family,
  That being, so gentle and brave ?
I know she never could fancy me,
  I'm but a fire Zouave.

" I'd show her my name upon my arm,
  My wounds and prospects lay bare,
I'd tell of my strength till her heart should warm
  If — I only had more hair.

" Methought, as I lay on my bed last night,
  Just as the moonbeams fell here,

She quietly stole upon my dim sight,
 And dropped on my hand a tear.

" And she murmured something of kindred love
 In such a pitying tone,
I thought the words which so deeply could move,
 Came not from her lips alone.

" And I thought, though this I scarce dare confess,
 For it could not, could not be,
That when she came my wounds to dress,
 She gave a kiss to me.

" ' Twas just as the clock had ceased its stroke
 Of the little hour of " one,"
I strove to detain her — but alas, I awoke,
 And the moonlight and she were gone.

" Would it were true, — she so kindly can weep,
 Why should I fear her then ?
Perhaps, if she thinks I am asleep,
 Why, may be, she'd kiss me again.

" Here goes ! " and back on his little bed
 In well-feigned sleep he lay,
And 'twas not long after sense had fled
 That the lady came that way.

And she saw in his true and sweet repose
 A mind full easy to sway,

While *his sighs strayed up and down his nose*
  Like elephants at play.

He listened, she gazed — he murmured, she wept,
  He spoke of a beautiful land,
While a strange emotion upon him crept,
  As a tear fell on his hand.

All throbbing, yet burning, yet quiet, yet now
  Is come the warm breath of bliss ;
For he feels a soft hand on his brow,
  And on his lips a kiss.

He sudden awakes, — she starts from his grasp,
  And fain would his presence flee,
But he held her firm, — so a locket and clasp
  She gave him to set her free.

She then disappeared ; while enraptured quite
  Regardless of pain or pelf,
The Zouave found in the locket so bright,
  A portrait of herself.

" Oh, joy ! here too a name is wrought, —
  'Tis Emma ! — burst not my heart —
When coming South, 'twas little I thought,
  The shaft of Love to start ! "

But now she comes with a firmer tread,
  And dancing eyes, where gaiety we trace,

Benevolence stands out upon her head,
    A Roman nose upon her face.

The Zouave looked upon her — saw her smile —
    He took her hand, — in whispers fine
And tremulous, without deceit or guile,
    He softly murmured, " Wilt be mine ? "

" Emma," said he, " thou'st done the greatest harm,
    The keenest flash thou did'st impart,
For though a bayonet ran through my arm,
    Thy eyes have pierced my heart."

She pressed his hand, — the story it is true, —
    And answered with a quiet glee,
" The same ball that has tortured you,
    Alack ! has wounded me ! "

" Then be thou mine, though angel innocence;
    For thee I'll fight, or beg, or steal ;
Be thou the only healing recompense
    That e'er my wounds shall feel."

" Not now," the maiden modestly replies,
    " Though often to thy bedside I'll be won,
The only union that I now dare recognize,
    Is that of Washington !

    " One day, when Fate has ceased these wars
        And men have ceased to bleed,

And thou acquired perhaps new scars,
   Then I'll be thine indeed !

" Farewell, farewell ! nor ever seem to know,
   Save only as a woman true,
She who through life would thy wife gladly go,
   Which now my country's need forbids to do."

The Zouave kissed her many kind adieus,
   And she withdrew, her mission to obey ;
So we'll suppose, when Peace her charm renews,
   That they'll be married in the usual way.

SONG.

The winter 's howling round us, boys,
   But our hearts are warming,
Soon, perhaps, the sound, my boys,
   Will hear of battle storming.
What care we for wassail wine ?
   Naught in those can cheer us,
What is like the " form in line,"
   When the battle's near us ?

CHORUS.—Here's to a soldier's life, my boys,
        Here's to a soldier's life !
        Here's to a soldier's strife my boys,
        The soldier's life and strife.

Bravely in the van, my boys,
   We will march together ;
" Charge," as none else can, my boys,
   In all kinds of weather.
For the life we love to sing,
   Which we e'er will cherish,
Is the soldier's, — so it bring
   Danger, though we perish.

4*

SONNET TO THE "NAMELESS ONES."

An Affecting Scene.   An interesting incident occurred on
Friday at the Baltimore station.   While the returning troops
were waiting to take the cars, one of the cavalry that had just
arrived, espied a brother in the ranks, and dismounting, ran to
embrace him.   As soon as the salutation was over, he inquired
of two other brothers, who had also been in the battle at Bull's
Run, and the reply was, "they are in their graves."   The
scene was so affecting that every bystander united their tears
with those of the weeping brothers.   They soon after took, perhaps, a final leave of each other — the one returning home
wounded, and the other proceeding to defend the honor and in-
tegrity of his Government.   These brothers were Germans,
and one of the dead was twin with the one that was entering the
army.—*Phil. Inquirer.*

"In their graves!" oh words of anguish
    Which a brother's tongue imparts;
Can our holy cause e'er languish,
    Breasted by such noble hearts?
"In their graves!" their forms attired
    In the solemn dress of woe;
But their souls, by God inspired,
    Shine with fame's intensest glow.
Brothers meeting — brothers speaking
    Of two brothers battle killed.
Brothers parting, — hearts a breaking,
    Though God of battles willed;
"In their graves!" — Oh God, restrain
    The bullets sent at these two who remain.

TO THE MEMORY OF A SENATOR SOLDIER.

Sadly the bells are tolling, tolling,
  Over the gloomed and surging streets ;
Slowly the drums are rolling, rolling,
  High above our own heart-beats.
Blackly the hearse is bearing, bearing,
  One to the open-laurelled tomb ;
Wildly the throng is wearing, wearing,
  Looks of fevered funeral-gloom ;
And the bells, and the drums, and the hearse, and
      the throng,
      And the voice from the bells,
      As it sighfully swells,
      And the moan from the drums
      As it deepfully comes,
      And the groans of each wheel
      Of the hearse as they steal,
      And the wails of the throng
      As they sob along,
  Usurping the heart and filling the eye,
  Tell us a great one is passing by,
  A last hour on earth is drawing nigh.

And the bells and the drums, and the hearse and
      the throng,
And the tributes they utter, — this heart-giving
      song,
To the memory of Baker shall ever belong.

TO THE DEAD HERO OF MISSOURI.

Lyon, we mourn! whose great unselfishness,
  Whose high devotion spoke of heaven's grace,
Whose bright career while weeping still we bless,
  Now thou art gone ! who, who, shall fill thy
    place ?
'Twas not enough that thou should'st give thy
    brain,
  With all its bright conceptions battle shown,
But thou must give thy life — yet not in vain
  Our country says, " thy fame is still her own."
Legions of armed men will think of thee,
  And rush from fireside joys to battle woes,
To plant the Eagle banner of the free
  Upon the graves of sin-stained rebel foes.
Lyon ! thou gav'st thy fortune and thy blood,
Fame calls thee to her glowing brotherhood.

THE SENTINEL AND I.

Sentinel ! Sentinel !
　Sentinel tall !
Pacing so quietly
　On the high wall,
Tell me, I pray,
　Whatever sight
Comes to your watchful eyes
　This silver night.
Tell me if ghostly
　Torments assail,
Tell me if wolfish
　Voices bewail,
Tell me if battle
　Urges its ply,
Tell me whate'er you see
　In the white sky !

FIRST REPLY —
　I see a peaceful valley lying,
　　Hugging close a crystal stream,
　A maiden, too, seems gently sighing
　　To the borders of a dream ;

Blue her eyes — her fond soul trembling
  Forth, in many a moonlight gem ;
Lips, whose blush (all charms resembling,)
  Tells me love-words hang on them.
Fair her form, — her bosom swelling
  Gently with the joys of peace,
That up to her eyes are welling
  From a bosom's soft release ;
And I see the streamlet winding
  Through the landscape's lovely scene,
And a rapture I am finding
  In the beauty of the scene.
Now she sinks with dove-like slumbering,
  While a sigh the soft air stirs,
For a band of angels, numbering
  Like to our Christ's ministers,
Float above her, sweetly sounding
  Lutes whose harmonies unite
With the voices now surrounding
  To instil a keen delight ;
And they leave her now with singing,
  (May such rich tones never cease,)
And the song they sing comes bringing
  These deep words : " This, this is peace,"
And the woods around are ringing
  With the whispered words of peace, —
    " This is the vale of Peace,
    And this the maid of Peace."

    Thank you, sir Sentinel,
    Sentinel tall !

Paeing so solemnly
    On the high wall;
Throwing a shadow down
    Awfully nigh,
Showing your form against
    Yon deepening sky.
Thank you, good Sentinel,
    Tallest of men !
Tell me what now you see,
    Look up again !
Find me some reason,
    By the moon's light,
Why you are pacing thus
    Through the long night !

SECOND REPLY. —
    Ah ! there is the valley and there the stream
        That lately I was praising,
    But the stream is a running pool of blood
        And the valley is all blazing.
    The trees and the fruits, fair flowers, the grass,
        Are seized with a vast decaying,
    While the heated, open-mouthed earth, alas !
        On the blood of men is preying.
    With a deadly impulse brothers meet,
        On a sister soil contending,
    While the parent weeps o'er her hope's defeat,
        For the land she has ceased defending.
    A monster appears by the bloody stream,
        Every nerve and musele straining,

As he stalks around with a deathly gleam
  And fire his red face veining.
Now! now he has seized a shrinking maid
  That from his wrath was fleeing,
Now he wipes anew his gory blade
  To murder that helpless being;
And now she falls on her woman knees,
  For a few days more appealing,
Now a lifting cloud of smoke she sees,
  A friendly host revealing;
And the monster, assailed on every side,
  A refuge now is seeking;
He startles the moving, glistening tide
  With his loud and horrid shrieking.
His yells and the shouts and the musketry
  Of the armies now engaging,
And the crackling flames and the hissing tree
  Tell me a battle is raging.
From flame and from hiss, from yell and from
      shout,
  A voice on my ear is preying,
It rises above the thunders about,
The screams of the battle's deadly rout.
      " This is war," the voice is saying,
  " This is war," is echoed in valleys,
      Over the tones of praying;
  " This is war," is told on the mountains
      Wherever a shepherd is straying.
  This is why on the granite ramparts
      On guard to-night I am staying.

Thank you, good Sentinel,
    Tallest of men!
Tell me more, Sentinel,
    Look up again!
Ask the blue heavens
    Once more to send,
Pictures to show you,
    When war will end.

THIRD REPLY. —
Again do I see the valley and stream,
            Enclosing
A village, all fresh in morning's first beam
            Reposing;
I see too the emblem of liberty
            So endearing.
Hail! hail to its folds, the flag of the free
            Is appearing.
The old stars and stripes, oh, ne'er may they cease
            Glory inviting,
Till treason is crushed 'neath the heel of a peace,
            Heaven alighting.

        Glory to God for it,
            Sentinel, shout!
        Glory to God for it,
            Let us both shout!
        Glory to the highest!
            Amen!

Good night, sir Sentinel,
   Let us both pray,
But " Glory to God " is all,
   All I can say.
Glory to God for it !
God bless McClellan !
   Glory to God !
      Amen !

SONNET ON A PEBBLE,

TAKEN FROM THE GRAVE OF STEPHEN A. DOUGLAS.

Weep, heart, at relic of the wondrous great!
   In whom command with music tones was blent,
Who seized his power from the hand of fate,
   And dealt in eloquence divinely sent.
Stilled is the voice that thrilled the Senate hall,
   Stilled is the hand held forth in mercy's cause,
Stilled is the heart that from the sky did fall
   To teach the grandest sovereignty of laws.
If but a simple uninscribed stone
   Starts from the eye the full unbidden tear,
How vastly more would be the worship shown,
   If his true, great, immortal self were here.
Oh, Douglas! death thy glory elevates,
For lo! thy resting place o'ertops the States.

ODE TO THE WAILING DOGS.

I.

What meant the blue of that meagre light,
   In the quiet depths of yonder room,
   And the solemn emblems of woful gloom,
As I looked on the fated house last night ?
        What meant that moan,
        In an undertone,
That came from the window over the street ?
        And the sudden throb
        Of that wailful sob
As it shot through my ears like a demon fleet !
  And why were the shutters almost closed ?
And why was the crape on the silent door ?
  'Twas because a being who once reposed
Within yon room shall repose no more ;
   Save only a rest which none can escape,
That quiet which comes when the pulse is fled.
  Ah ! that is the cause of the swinging crape
Ah ! truly and bitterly some one is dead,
Yes ! one of the choicest of spirits has fled,
     That ever a family circle knew,
       Ah ! bitterly true,
One of that household is cold and dead.

II.

Ah! what was that howling, the night before last,
   That I heard from the setting of sun to the morn,
That through the long night such an echo cast
   That it seemed the revels, ghosted forlorn,
   Of suffering spirits blighted and torn?
      That startled it seemed forever,
      With its sharp infernal quiver
      Dipped in some saturnal river
   The pulsations of that night,
      With such a dismal groan,
That my soul grew sick of the long afright
And each piercing shriek then seemed my own.

III.

Now, now I remember, it has often been said
That ere a spirit of man has fled,
That a dog will under the window creep,
Where the suffering body labors to sleep
At night, and rend the air with his song
Of myriad howls, keen moanings and long.
Why is the brute so endowed with sense,
   To know beforehand when to grieve?
Why should *he* waft a spirit hence,
   And we in a death so disbelieve?

IV.

And now I know why I creep to-night,
With the dull, damp chill of a dizzy fright,
As I list to the howls of the storm without,

As I list to the moans of the brutes about.
  The sun to-day, nor martial, nor proud,
Planted a red and sickening dearth,
On the joyous gush of my rising mirth,
  And left a robe of storm-like cloud,
To embrace the form of the darkened earth.
Oh, list to the moaning catalogues!
    Which prey upon the ear,
    And fill the heart with fear,
    Sounding far, and sounding near,
    As they wail their souls away,
    Making me like statue clay,
    And I wish 'twere dawn of day.
      Oh, the moaning
      And the groaning
Of the bed-forsaking dogs.
Of the dread awaking dogs.

V.

And one is a kind of suffering groan,
And one a kind of a sobbing moan,
And one starts up like a shriek of affright
And sounds unto the ears of the night,
    Like the crack of a bursting zone.
While one is a deep entrumpeted sigh,
And one a fond and sorrowing cry,
That steals away to the dusky sky,
    Following perhaps his master home.
Oh, who can tell me the reason why,
    These voices madly come?

These strainings,
And complainings
Of the sin inspiring dogs,
Of those inexpiring dogs ;
These throbbings,
And the sobbings,
Of the fever sending dogs,
Of the never ending dogs,
Why do they madly come?

VI.

Now over rills, and clover hills,
Come these maddening, saddening ills ;
From sorrel sheaves, and laurel leaves
A leaping, creeping mystery, weaves,
Its horrid game
Of torrid flame,
With its list of memories ever the same
O'er every part of my weeping heart
That beats in this panting frame.
In the far off distance,
By the sharp assistance,
Of a quivering ear, and a shivering fear,
Such sounds I hear,
That they make me think
Till I ache and sink,
That they are the shrieking voices fled,
From the tombs of the doubly damnéd dead ;
Who once in a hundred centuries,
Are allowed to tell their injuries,

And revel in moon-stricken vagaries
Without interdiction.
And now in the thundered screamings
Comes the woe of a thousand dreamings,
Of Satan's infliction,
In the clashing of the teeth,
In the gnashing of the teeth,
In the chillings, and the thrillings,
Of the heart a wringing dogs,
Of the dart a-flinging dogs.

VII.

Where never a breath is,
There ever a death is,
Be it in gloomy deserted hall,
Be it on roomy, mould-skirted wall,
Be it in swamp,
Or be it in fen,
Be it in camp,
Or be it in men,
Be it in forest or be it in lair,
Be it on crag-top, jagged and bare,
Be it on ocean, waveless and glossy,
Be it on battle-field, graveless and mossy,
Be it in fear moans,
Be it in brave souls,
Be it in dear tones,
Be it in grave holes,
Be it 'mong people under the earth,
The things of the roving air,

It comes with a chill to freeze our mirth,
  Like the iceberg touch of care.
And so do these night air demagogues,
Those eternal nightmare giving dogs,
Chill with the doeful news,
Breathed on the breath of dampful dews.
  That some one is dead,
  Some loved one is dead,
  That many are dead,
  Many loved ones are dead,
And the heart grows sad with the doleful news,
  That comes in the sighing,
  That comes in the crying,
  Of the fear caressing dogs,
  Of the ear oppressing dogs.

VIII.

Oh, why do so many howl to-night?
  Has a battle been fought,
  That so many evil threats are fraught,
With the tones of death and blight?
Has vile disease wild scattered his damp
O'er the soldier on guard, on the march, or in camp?
Has a fever usurped the pulses bold,
Until their forms are a lying cold?
Has thirst, starvation, or accident,
Stolen many a soul from its tenement?
Have many been shot for orders ignored?
Or drowned while passing a river's ford?
Or poisoned by an enemy spy?

5

Or killed by a bursting missile nigh ?
Or have they died in a lingering fit ?
Or fallen by murderous comrade hit ?
Or shattered by a magazine blast ?
Or crisped by hot shot rebel cast ?
  That so many dogs should be pining,
  That so many dogs should be whining,
    That the heedless baying dogs,
    That the needless staying dogs,
    That the chills a-breeding dogs,
    That the ills a-feeding dogs,
      Should be howling,
      And be growling,
  With their tear a-wringing woes,
  With their ear a-stinging woes ?

IX.

Still, still their moans in my ears I find,
    Still, still they banish sleep,
    What can I do but weep,
    While my pulses curdle and creep,
While *they* still shriek to the howling wind ?
  Oh ! list to the wailful catalogue,
  That on my heart with a Condor clutch,
  And the cold chill of an adder touch
    Sit with a leaden sway.
  And the ghosten spell-bound dogs,
  And the coasten hell-hound dogs,
    Glooms the coming of the day.
  Oh, ye breast annoying dogs !

Oh, ye rest-destroying dogs !
    Take your tireless throats away,
    Ere maddened I turn gray,
And thought becomes the racking brain whirl's
    prey.

WHAT OUR WILLIE WOULD DO.

Would you be a soldier, Willie?
   And with the army go
To protect your country's flag, boy,
   And whip the upstart foe?
     Would you, boy?

Could you hold a musket, Willie,
   For hours in the line?
Could you wield a sword in battle, boy,
   With those tiny hands of thine?
     Could you, boy?

Would you know a rebel, Willie,
   If you saw him in the night?
Would you know his dress and looks, boy,
   With those little eyes so bright?
     Would you, boy?

Could you march a whole day, Willie,
   Through sand and woods and mire?

Through heat, and cold, and wet, boy,
    And your little feet ne'er tire ?
      Could you, boy ?

Would you not grow faint, my Willie ?
    And your little post resign ?
Would you not grow sick and sore, boy,
    With a frame so frail as thine ?
      Would you not ?

WILLIE'S REPLY.—
    Yes, I wish I were a soldier,
      With a plumed hat of taste,
    And a sword upon my side, Whit. !
      And a sash around my waist.
    I would go into the South, sir,
      And make a deal of noise,
    Then draw out my little sword, Whit.,
      And fight the little boys.
        Yes, I could,
        And I would.

THE UNITED STATES BLACKSMITH SHOP.

St. Tristam rules the army,
　McClellan is a rogue,
For he allows that wickedness
　In camps is much in vogue.

By strictest regulations,
　He tires many felloes,
And then he tries to raise the wind,
　By working at a Bellows.

And then he drafts a workman,
　A musketeer or rammer,
And never checks the action
　Of forging with a hammer.

His army for his presence
　No gratitude e'er feels,
Because, on his compulsion,
　They made so many " wheels."

Himself can take the gilt off
　Any jockey on the course,

Because he can so daintily,
    And often, shoe a horse.

His workmen are a'species
    Of thieves, (I speak in fun),
Because you see they're guilty
    Of often steeling iron.

At Bull's Run they were cowards,
    And well-nigh lost a steak ;
McDowell made a fire,
    The rebels made a " break.'

McClellan has a fashion
    Of smiling iron smiles,
And he takes the rebel's brass off
    By using of his files.

He saves his own head cutely,
    Though not all through fear,
And gives the enemy a slap,
    By *falling on his rear.*

Oh wonderful effort of genius !
    Oh stubborn mettle of will !
What can excel the thrilling feat ?
    He *puts a file throngh a drill !*

What need, when so many workmen
    His shops are teeming with —

What need, I say, of another,
And he, a General Smith ? —

Who has a system of working,
As every General should, —
He *nails* the rebels by *driving*
  · *Their soldiers into the wood.*

Success to our Smithy so clever !
His danger he truly feels,
For under " cover " he places
A body subject to wheels.

Instead of giving the rebels,
Which ne'er their coffer fills,
Hard dollars and cents, he gives them
Nothing but gunpowder *mills.*

Success to our army and navy,—
A blessing I invoke,
That none of the fires they ever make,
May ever end in smoke.

THE SOLDIER'S FUNERAL.

See the solemn pacings, pacings,
　Of the people as they mourn,
See the grief-pale facings, facings,
　Of the soldiers all forlorn ;
See them pacing to the vault,
See them facing to the vault,
To the cold, eternal vault,
To the sad and dripping vault ;
Where the many mazy tracings
　On the mould upon the wall,
And the web-like interlacings
　Of the worm trails on the wall,
　The damp and glistening tracings
Cover coffins, bones and pall,
Cover stones and mould and all.

And the heavy sighings, sighings,
　Shaking every anxious frame,
And the soul-throb cryings, cryings,
　Starting like a smothered flame,
　Writhing like a pent-up flame,
　　5*

Like a blasting, chilling flame
From the caverns of the dead,
With a dreadful lustre shed,
Speak the never-ending fame
Of the illustrious dead !
Speaking with a gasping breath
Of the fiery hand of death,
Speaking with a broken voice,
Of the nation's stricken choice.

And when we strain our eyes
Along the street of sighs,
Naught but mourning signs we see,
Naught but warning sighs we hear,
Naught but earthly sorrow comes ;
For the voices of the drums,
Muffling with their solemn beats,
Our souls up in their beats,
The chant-like moaning beats,
Of the muffled rolling drums,
Chills on every living breath,
With the solemn thought of death ;
Saying, every living breath,
Must soon prepare for death.

BEN BRONT'S RETRIBUTION.

All day the surging battle's roar,
   And dreadful havoc's ply,
Had rolled upon the shivering earth,
   One great heart-rending cry ;
From bleeding bosoms faintly came
   Life's separating sigh.

One Captain still unwearied fights,
   Still leads his company,
Now heading in the dangerous van,
   Now halting steadily,
While rifle, bomb, and cannon ball,
   Fall fast and greedily.

One man still hugs his rifle close,
   Still presses to the front,
Still watches for the moment when
   No eyes but his are on't ;
And then that stain shall be wiped out,
   The man is brave Ben Bront.

Around full many wounded men
   In bloody garments lay,
Some clutching tight their muskets bright,
   As though their strength to try;
Some glaring at the upraised hoof
   With terror in their eye.

Some leaning on one elbow, pale
   As any coffined shroud,
With parched lips and dull, white tongue,
   Moan out a prayer aloud,
That He, the God of battles, will
   Remove this bloody cloud.

Some grown mad with the angry fang
   That teethes upon their brain,
Howl forth in curses, that no ease
   Comes for the storm of pain,
That gives each nerve consuming pangs,
   Which makes them howl again.

While others, with their limbs shot off,
   A little water crave ;
While others, sightless, bite the earth,
   And call on it to save, —
Ne'er thinking if that succor comes,
   It comes but in the grave.

But see the charge! — Oh, yonder battery,
   With it's terrific fire,

Has long enough it's thunder-doom of death
  Pronounced on son and sire,
Has long enough seethed forth in hellish sport,
  Annihilation dire.

Ben mutters to himself — " my time has come,
  And so, I think, is his,
Farewell then cringeling ! " now it is " take aim."
Now " fire," and fire it is. —
" By heaven ! I've hit him, — yes, he falls ! " —
One leaps the reins to seize.

But Ben with deeper aim springs forth
  Nor thinks he of remorse
To him who, with one sickening swoon,
  Reels dead-like from his horse ;
Who soon will answer for his crimes
  Within Ben's arms, a corse.

And then Ben's comrade and himself,
  The Captain quickly bore
To yonder tree, and begged the shade,
  Far from the cannon's roar;
While all the while the Captain's face
  A rigid, death-look wore.

" Here's water, Captain, rouse thee, man !
  Nay, let it not be said
That you succumbed to the first touch
  Of dull and lifeless lead ;

Come, rouse thee, Captain ! nor put on
   That look of the clammy dead.

" Run, comrade ! pray the surgeon find,
   He bids thee with his moan ;
I've plenty here to ease his pain,
   Go ! I will stay alone,
And bathe the hot and swollen neck,
   Perchance 'twill check a groan."

The soldier started at full speed
   The mission to perform ;
The Captain slowly ope'd his eyes,
   His cheeks grew slowly warm ;
And Ben sat sternly waiting for
   The rising of the storm. —

A sad, sad thought, the soul of which
   Was moulded by despair,
Stood in the brimful vacancy
   Of that unsteady stare,
As looking up, the Captain speaks,
   " Where am I ? tell me, where ? "

" Not far from where the bloody work, —
   Nay, do not seek to rise !
I'll tell thee all, — that charge is made,
   The enemy now flies;
But, Captain, fainter still thy breath,
   And glassier seem thy eyes,"

" No ! no ! I'm strong yet, yet fearing much —
 Are we alone, — are we ?
I'm very weak — my neck it burns !
 Can'st thou a wound e're see ? —
But yet this blood, that trickles down.
 It must belong to me ! "

" Yes, Captain, yes ! a great deep wound
 By Minie ball I find ;
All through the neck it must have gone,
 On it my sash I'll bind,
But, strange to say, the murderous ball
 Did enter from behind.

" Hast thou no message to a friend,
 Whom for thy fate will weep ?
No loving wife within whose arms
 Thoud'st wish to fall asleep ?
If so, make haste ! e'en now I see,
 Death's tremors on thee creep."

" Yes !" faintly said the dying man,
 " My Ellen ! " gasped he, " You
Will remember me to her,
 And give my fond adieu."
" Thy Ellen, sir !" cried Ben " is't so ?
 Hast thou an Ellen, too ?

" Yes, yes, a dear one, tell her where
 I died, and tell her how,

With demon hands upon my neck
 But an angel's on my brow.
And tell her that I always loved,
 And still do love her now."

" I'll tell her Captain, all, and faithfully,
 And start ere close of day.
Is it not strange that we two are alone,
 Both powerless to pray ?
Bethink thee, Captain, is there nothing more,
 That thou would'st like to say ?

" Yes, yes — my boy, four summers old,
 With curly golden hair —
His portrait — her's too — fondly clasped
 I, in my bosom bear,
Pray take them out and say to her
 I loved to have them there."

" I'll tell her Captain, all and faithfully,
 But yet I do repine,
That whil'st thy Ellen is so favored with
 Warm sentiments and fine,
That in thy dying rhapsodies
 Thou hast forgotten *mine*."

" Thine — what of thine ? " the dying moaned.
 Said Ben, " I much regret
That thou, who once did vow to love,
 Could thus so soon forget,

My wife, whose ruin once ye sought,
  Told me, my rage to whet."

"I'll tell *thy* Ellen of *that* too,
  And with a horrid glee,
I'll say it was *my bullet,* sir,
  That set thy spirit free.
So much sir, for thy freedom with,
  The wife who clings to me."

" No, no! not that, thou demon brute,
  Nor think that yet I'll die,
Beware thee, fiend! for I intend
  Thy boasted strength to try.
By heavens, are my weapons gone?
  I thought I had them nigh."

"Ah, ha!" cried Ben, " don't think I'd trust,
  My life in hands of thine,
I took the pistols from thy belt,
  And put them into mine.
Ah, ha! my Captain, did I right
  To put them into mine?"

The Captain with a savage howl,
  Of dreadful hate and pain,
Rushed towards Ben, and blindly kicked,
  And yelled and struck again;
While all the time a bloody stream,
  Gushed from his neck, amain.

At last upon the grassy ground,
  His spenten form he threw,
Gnawed till he died a Beechen tree,
  That very near him grew ;
While the guns of the distant battle,
  Roared a terrible adieu.

" Dead, dead ! "   said Ben, " I forgive him.
  His, now is a sacred trust,
His last request was so loving,
  So tender a charge, that I must."
Ben took out the portraits, and kissed them,
  And dropped a tear in the dust.

THE SOLDIER'S RETURN.

INSCRIBED TO THE THREE MONTHS' VOLUNTEERS.

Home again ! and hearts are lightened,
   From the dusks of war emerging;
All the clouds of love are tightened,
   To the bonds eternal verging.
Songs that late were sung in sadness
   To employ the gloomy hour,
Burst with chorus full of gladness,
   To the height of gushing power.

Home again ! with hands uplifted,
   The wife a song to God is wreathing,
While her eager eye is gifted
   With the honeyed words, love's wreathing;
And her form is now encircled,
   With the brawny arms and strong,
And her lips are now enpurpled,
   With a hearty kiss and long.

Home again ! with hands united,
   In a lisping circle forming,

With panting bosoms, eyes all lighted,
　To welcome from the battles storming,
A father dear, from States benighted,
　Where treason's folly sways each hour,
But whose troops shall start affrighted,
　When is hurled the bolts of power.

Home again ! the lonely-hearted
　Unkinned soldier, sadly peering
On the scenes which late had started
　All the throbs for charms endearing,
Moves along, no home invites him,
　Workshops empty, men complaining,
Naught there is of love excites him,
　None but dins of wars remaining.

Ah, the leaping forms all trembling,
　Good right hands so keenly wringing,
Tell us there is no dissembling,
　No regret a shade is flinging.
All around some consolation,
　To his asking soul is starting,
Of those friends, whose deep laudation,
　Has repaid the woe of parting.

Home again ! and souls are freighted,
　With an interest each exciting,
And the eyes that long have waited
　Glisten with a joyous lighting :

Pangs across the heart have started,
  When the thoughts of battle come,
But the blood of joy has started,
  For the soldier now is home.

THE SOLDIER LOVER'S PARTING.

Come, strike a hand with mine, love !
  Come, strike a hand with mine ;
And let the warm beats of this breast
  Now nestle into thine.
For I see a tear of sorrow, love,
  Doth in thy soft eyes shine,
So let us strike our hands, love,
  Come strike a hand with mine !

Come, press your lips to mine, love,
  Come, press your lips to mine ;
And with one voice we'll ask of Him
  Supporting grace divine,
A soul of light so holy, love,
  Now in thine eye doth shine,
I feel its warm breath on the lips
  Now pressed so close to mine !

JOY TO THE DEAD.

INSCRIBED TO THE MEMORY OF THAT GALLANT SOL-
DIER, ELMER E. ELLSWORTH.

Oh, see ye that lady a-mourning,
    Over the grassless mound,
The eyes of the world a-scorning,
    In the depths of her grief profound?
Oh, see ye the hands that are wringing,
    Dipped deeply in sorrow's cup ?
Oh, see ye the love that is clinging?
    The tears that the earth drinks up?
Do you hear that terrible throbbing ? —
    Ye may well, for still is the air ;
Do ye list to the painful throbbing
    That comes from the lady there ?
Then down on your knees for giving
    A prayer to the king of the dead,
And these righteous words be giving,
    " Peace to the solemn dead.
And peace to the sorrowful living,
    And peace to the soldier dead."

What, if that voice should reach him ?
What, if that grief he should know ?
What, if those tears should teach him,
The States are sorrowing so ?
What, if our prayers should move him,
To believe in a deathless name ?
To believe that the States now love him,
As one of Immortal fame ?
Would his eyes not start with a gushing flame ?
And his heart renew its fire ?
Would his frame not pant as of old, the same ?
And his lofty soul aspire ?

Do the dead ever weep,
In that solemn sleep ?
Do touches of life through their body creep,
If words of love
Come to their ears from the world above ?
Do the dreadful woes
Of stricken foes,
Ever make them *smile* in their deep repose ?
Do the joys confessed,
In a dear friend's breast
Make them content in the coffin's rest ?
Who, who of the living can ever know,
If these unearthly things are so ?
Ah, if we knew
It were only true,
That after this little breath were gone,

And over our forms were planted a stone,
  We should know indeed
  Whose heart would bleed,
Whose voice would utter the keenest moan
  That we were gone,
Perhaps we would look more friendly on death,
  Nor struggle so terribly,
  Nor writhe so horribly,
To retain yet longer our waning breath.
   But no one can tell,
   If a heart will swell
   With the pangs of grief,
   Or if eyes will pour
   Their briny store,
   In sorrow's relief;
   And so we avoid
   The terrible nod
Of Him who places us under the sod,
   And shudder and moan,
   And struggle and groan
   And sometimes curse,
   If a thought of the hearse
Comes bearing us off to the grave alone.

   But the lustre shed,
   From the soldier dead,
   Tells over his form.
   There comes a storm
    Of national wailing,

When the tear-capped clouds are splendidly reft,
And his beaming glory, alone, is left,
   In the sun's rays unfailing ;
And the living shall share with the dead the fame,
Immortal honor sheds on Ellsworth name.

A LAMENT FROM FORT LAFAYETTE.

Cold blows the wind across the bay,
  And how it hums about
The casements, all this dreary day,
  To check each purposed shout!
List! how it moans again — I fear
  That I must soon resign it;
I dread to know its presence here,
  Lest Lincoln should confine it!

I gaze out on the hazy sea
  With such a longing eye,
I see the birds so lithe and free
  Between me and the sky.
A drifting log, yon frigate black,
  The giddy, floundering fish —
All, all are free; but I, alack,
  For freedom can but wish.

'Tis true, I would have done a wrong
  To that flag waving o'er me,

And stabbed the hand so fond and strong,
  That unto riches bore me.
But yet I scarcely think it's fair
  Such rigid walls should bind me ;
Oh ! had I wings to cleave the air,
  Soon would they gleam behind me.

But farewell, Freedom ! till these wars
  Have ceased their bloody reign ;
Perhaps, I yet shall heaven's stars
  Hail in my home again.
Farewell, my deeds in Honor's name !
  My heart's ambitious swell !
But thou of very life, the flame,
  Sweet Freedom ! still, farewell !

THE GRAVE DIGGER OF MANASSAS AT MIDNIGHT.

Eighteen hours to-day again !
    Eighteen hours to-day
Have I toiled at this dismal business,
Till I'm almost worked to craziness,
    Hiding the motionless clay ;
And hundreds are unburied yet,
And my muscles are stiff and clammy, and wet —
    Oh, for a streak of restful day !

Eighteen hours to-day again !
    Eighteen hours to-day,
Have I piled in together my foe, and my friend,
And yet seem no nearer my labor's end
    Than I was at the morn's first ray ;
Tossing into the ground my kind,
Until I am sick, and almost blind,
    Yet not a word dare say.
Just now a shade from the moon came down,
Seeming to cast a deep, sullen frown,
    And I weep on my spade my soul away.

Can ever a God-hope brighten this scene,
Brighten this dark and gloomy ravine ?
    Or the sun, with a special ray ?

  Eighteen hours to-day again!
    Eighteen hours to-day ;
And I still must dig, spite the pain at my side,
If only yon gaping corpses to hide,
    The battle's hideous prey.
Just now a chill o'er my frame did creep,
I fear I must, though I dread to sleep,
    Though there's none alive to betray.
Hark ! to the moanings filling the air,
Seeming to come from yon shadows there,
    Of spectres, of green and gray.
And yet ! oh yet ! I am not done
Though some distant clock is striking one ! —
    When can I stop to pray ?

There's the fiftieth man I have put to his rest,
With his shrivelled hands folded over his breast,
    In the tenderest way ;
And yet no relief ! I fear I'm forgot, —
They have sent me here to die, and to rot !
    What a fearful game to play !
But this half-covered form I'll let alone,
To search out the cause of that ghostly groan,
    Which thumps in my ears away ;
So I'll lay down the spade, and walk around,

To search out the cause of the fearful sound
    That seems just near me to stay !

  Eighteen hours to-day again !
    Eighteen hours to-day !
Oh ! would I were back in my home, by the side
Of dear, blooming May, my loving young bride,
    Who three weeks ago did say,
" Go forth, my pride, with a willing hand,
And help to defend our native land
    From those who'd betray ! "
Pshaw ! these tears ! but look, look ! look there !
At that fiery serpent, twisting in air !
    What weapon have I to slay ?
I'd take my spade, but 'tis covered with slime,
And my pick is used in a work of crime,
    'Tis digging my brains away !

And thick grows the air, with a murky green ;
Ha ! ha ! how I laugh, for I cannot be seen,
    To be made the prey
Of that leaping, hissing demon there, —
Yet he comes ! now nearer ! give me some air !
    How shall I get away ?
Nearer he comes ! is there no way to save ?
Ah, ha ! *that last and but half-filled grave*,
    In there I'll get and pray ;
Quickly I'll onward, he's coming so fast !
The time for escape will soon be past,
    And he will scorch me for play !

Now I am in! — ugh! what a chill
Dwells in the body lying so still,
    With him *must I stay*,
Through the long night? Yes! for that shout
Tells there's no time for turning him out,
    He, the harmless clay.
Quickly, man! in with the dirt! — why so loth?
Now there's enough to cover us both
    If moveless we stay;
Quick! let us hide from the green flaming eye;
Put your arm over me — so, as we lie;
    So, — let us pray!

Why do you shake so? boldly, good sir!
There's a terrible risk in the least little stir,
    Do you hear what I say?
Do you think that I am at all afraid,
Because I am coldly, cozily laid
    In this ravine away?

Ah! little thought I, when at work alone,
That the fiftieth grave I dug was my own;
    What a jest, I say;
But mortals outside, as you but now said,
Know little of jokes, that start out of us dead,
    When the demons are away.

But I grow very chilly; pray spare me your coat,
And wrap your warm sash around my damp throat,

Oh, hurry, I pray !
There now, I am ready, and I list the command,
It is God's saying, come to my beautiful land.
Good bye ! — I am marching away.

ADDRESS TO A REBEL TOE NAIL,

WHICH CAME FROM THE FOOT OF A SECESSIONIST WHO FOUGHT
AT SPRINGFIELD AND LEXINGTON.

Horny rascality !
From a locality
Where no hilarity
    Lightens the brain ;
Let me look at thee !
Sure sin begat thee !
Strove to enfat thee,
    On rebel grain !

Dirty and grimy,
Rugged and slimy ;
Fearfully nigh me,
    Who was it bore thee ?
Smelling offensively,
Unpared extensively,
Throwing expensively,
    Perfumes all o'er me !
What was it started thee ?
Who was it parted thee ?

6*

Who was it carted thee
From thy dear toe ?
Was't sword stroke of Lyon,
Was't bullet too nigh on
The toe thou did'st die on ?
Oh ! What was thy woe ?

Did some foul diseasing,
With pains unappeasing,
Strive for the releasing
Of thee from thy place?
Did some huge man frantic,
In colossal antic,
In deed unromantic
Tread on thy face ?

Perhaps in a thicket.
When playing at " Picket "
Thy owner did'st kick it
Against some rude stump ;
Which (most likely story)
Taught him the glory
Of stump oratory
All in a lump.

Shade of Missouri !
Fain I'd allure thee
With strains of " Pot Pouri "
But I desist me !
Knowing thy feelings well,

Scorning thy dealings well,
Hissing thy stealings well,
       So I resist me!

Solemn decaying,
On thee is weighing,
Heavily preying
       On thy life's core!
So all rebellious things,
Man, beast, (secessious things)
Shall be oblivious things,
       Counting no more,
Than a dead stock in hand,
Than a crushed rock in hand,
Than a burnt block in hand,
       Which none deplore.
Farewell! grime of Hessian!
Thou horn of oppression!
Thou nail of secession!
       Thy mission is o'er.

A PICTURE OF WAR.

Ere dread calamity became the star,
The ruling God of nations, and of War;
Ere the fleet steed loud snorting to the wind,
Plunged on the foe and never looked behind;
Or ere with pious thrust, a reverend sire,
Proved words of peace consort with deeds of fire;
Ere heaving tempests lurked in caves of brass;
Or powder plots were ranged 'neath plains of grass;
Ere armed vessels groaned on ocean's breath,
To lightning forth the thunder tone of death;
Ere tumult swung aloft its banner torn,
And shrieked and swayed from gloomy morn to
        morn,
The world with tuneful cadences was filled,
In songs of praise all other sounds were stilled.

No voice of rage, in discords loud and shrill,
Piped its hot breath to breed a world of ill;
No tones of envy, most malicious power!
Scorched the fair day or gnawed upon the hour;

No fragile form fled from the assassin's knife,
Or begged in piteous tones a harmless life ;
No giant stride of hate, no shrink of fear,
Ere blanched the cheek or palled upon the ear ;
No robber crept beneath the robes of night ;
No piles of treasure ached upon his sight ;
Fell Rumor ne'er engrossed the gossip's care,
No virtue known, because no vice was there ;
The placid world hailed to the heavens above,
And challenged her white face, for all was peace
     and love.

Behold the spot where War colossal reigns,
On throne of fire, 'neath canopy of chains ;
His chieftains ranged about him, wait his nod,
Rage, pain, tears, rancour, torture, chilly sod,
Theft, violation, murder, endless harms,
With flaming eyeballs, and with ready arms.
Around him rise the black, uneven walls,
Decked o'er by demon skill, that sight appals ;
The walls themselves, the curious figures too,
The kingly throne, the horns the demons blew,
The numerous rattling canopies of state,
The chairs on which the grim attendants wait,
The urns in which the dread recordings lie,
The dome all tapestried, the carvings nigh,
The furniture, the seeming inlaid stones,
Were but a mass of wrought up human bones,
And when the Thunderer speaks, as speak he will,
And bellows loudly " Slaves, go forth and kill,"

The walls grow cold as though 'twere they to die,
And bone 'gainst bone, then chatters in reply.

In each dusk corner see a giant rise,
With bloody hands, and red-hot flaming eyes,
Eager to seize the the devastating brand,
And hurl destruction o'er a peaceful land ;
Half hid in chains, grown weak from mould and
          rust,
And hair all gray with damp sepulchral dust,
As though just from a century's carouse
In some extended, aged, charnel house.

First came dark Hate with nervous, darting look
Which the soft eye of love could never brook,
Whose deeds are first on chronicles accurst,
With one tremendous wrench his chains he burst.
His pondrous head, herculean form
Nor fears the thunder and defies the storm ;
His voice a tempest, and each movement death,
Scorpions and snakes lie hidden in his breath,
And thus he stands, a bolt of smothered harms —
No weapon has he but his mighty arms.
Bends he full low his master to allure,
That he a bloodier mission may secure.
Anon the great commander speaks in tones,
That startle with affright the rattling bones.
" Go forth thou minister of civil broil,
Range o'er the realms of gold the hut of toil,
Assail the planter in his sunny home,

Assail the merchant, 'neath his festive dome ;
By hasty act and venomed word of mouth,
Array the North 'gainst the feebler South ;
Embitter man 'gainst man, and will 'gainst will,
And soon I'll send a messenger to kill.
" Avaunt ! and haste thee," straightway giant Hate
Howled an adieu, and never stopped to prate.

Next Bloodshed came ; all scarred and singed his
      face.
As though by former deeds, he'd carved his place ;
Adown his arm the sword stroke furrows ran,
And all his limbs, the great seams deeply span ;
His eyebrows wore a black and rugged frown,
And from his mouth the blood-drops trickled down ;
Forth from his bloodshot eye, burst balls of fire,
That told of hellish deeds of vengeful ire.

No sooner had he shown his red-veined face,
Than his chains fell, blood-rusted from their place ;
He stamped and shook himself, as though to see
If all his functions were at liberty.
With a deep breath he made the place resound
And fell before his master with a bound.

" Hail sire ! potential God ! " he said ;
" At thy command I hither hasty speed ;
Released from fettered ease, I craving ask
That very soon thou'lt speak my baneful task."

" Give me thy hand, thou minister of blood ; "
And they embraced as kindred spirits should.
" Thy task it is the mighty sword to wield,
And scatter carnage on the battle-field ;
To fill with gaping wounds contending foes ;
To drown the national in domestic woes ;
To make the wolf draw nigh, the vulture stare,
At the big feast which thou wilt thus prepare.
Swing thy red sword until the vultures croak ;
Lop off the heads, a hundred at a stroke,
Until the earth, all sated with the gore
Rolls it away, refusing to drink more ;
Then hew, and hack, nor stop to talk or dream,
Till 'gins to swell like veins, each running stream ;
Nor cease thy work, till o'er the banks they flood,
And men, and land, and waters, all are blood."
Whetting his sword against a polished bone,
Dark Bloodshed leaped, and straightway he was
        gone.

Then greedy Rapine stole upon the scene,
And looked around, above bones, and between ;
Dark cunning flashed from his far sunken eye,
Where cruelty in dogged fear doth lie ;
Long arms, and mighty, move the soul to fright,
Like the grim rocks which fret the sea by night ;
Capacious yawning, hideous jaws
Tell of his nature by definéd laws ;

Limbs made for fleetness, strength, and stubborness
An anxious sense, all quivering, confess.

" Come hither, worthy slave ! thy sire, Theft,
Said if I watched thee not, naught would be left ;
And lest there's nothing else of thee remains,
Come in my own hands, place thy captive chains."
Thus War said, Rapine wished himself away,
Took up his chains, and hastened to obey.

" Thou know'st thy mission, double-limbed knave !
Forth to thy work, nor spare the church, nor grave ;
Creep with thy minions to the city's wealth,
Possess it or by knife, or fraud, or stealth ;
Pause at the rustic's door, for alms appeal,
Watch when he turns, then boldly in and steal ;
The maiden standing by the bowered gate
Steal thou away and boldly violate ;
The wife, who hides her husband's little hoard,
Knock on the head and seize on all that's stored ;
Trip up the workmen as they homeward go,
Filch the week's wages, war costs much you know ;
Throughout the land each town or rustic village,
Has too much wealth, 'twill lesser grow by pillage ;
Go forth ! and spare nor age, nor sex, nor kind,
Something from all, to bring away , thou'lt find ;
The mershant's marble palace, yielding farms,
The student's chamber, and the young girl's charms.
The beds of gold, the red and glowing wine,

Go bring them here, for I would have all mine."
Gathering his imps that soon around him flew
Rapine made his obeisance and withdrew.

With gaunt, yet fiery aspect then appeared,
Foul Devastation, guilt and blood besmeared;
Brimful of some fell purposed horrid woe,
Death in his look, which kills without a blow;
Huge limbs in some saturnal region born,
Bore up a frame which dooms mankind to mourn;
Stiff bristling from his thick uncovered neck,
Grew hairy swords, that drive the world awreck;
Upon his head the myriad tortures grew,
In heaving flames now burning darkly blue;
Disaster couchéd in his eager eyes,
And from his mouth the leaping torments rise;
A clot-stained sword he clutches in one hand,
The other swings aloft a burning brand;
Full twenty daggers grace his body belt,
Whose hackings show the blows he must have
        dealt.
Raging, he bellows and but ill at ease,
Before his chieftain, drops upon his knees.

War, smiling grimly, into greetings broke,
And to the kneeling slayer thus he spoke; —

" Hail, chiefest fiend ! all things above, below,
The fruits of thy good working, plainly show;
Thou'rt felt in dread consumption's ghastly sway;

In weeks on seas ; in mental strength decay ;
In the proud tree, low bending to the blast,
That with a crash falls to the ground at last ;
In castles, which the feudal flag unfurled
Now ruined, that had once defied the world ;
In the recoiling stroke of lightning flash,
Which over mountains, into forests crash ;
In storms, that rend the quiet farmer's hearth,
Uproot the trees, and barren make the earth ;
In flouting treason's pale ambiguous eye ;
In by-gone glory, and in patriot sigh.
Up and away, my friend and true,
Do all that Bloodshed, Hate and Rapine fear to
    do."

War, wishing to assist his friends afar,
Seized a huge sword, and bids his hosts " prepare."
" Charge on the world with double-hellish will,
And make it red with blood from those ye kill."
War said, and soon in battle line arrayed,
He bid his followers kiss his battle blade ;
Then with dread myriad howls they turned to go,
And drenched the world with one terrific blow.

LINES ON THE PROSPECT OF A WAR WITH ENGLAND.

England, England, stay thy hand !
Never in a fatal deed, let its power be put forth
To subdue the gallant spirts that attend upon the
   North,
  Sworn, a sacrificing band.

England, stay thy fancied might !
'Twill but dye old plains anew, with thy heroes'
   goodly blood,
'Twill but run the streams again with a red and
   clotted flood,
  Dyeing, running, day and night.

Eagles, ever swoop above
The creatures of the ground, be they lions, bears
   or snakes,
Denizens of forest acres, hissing monarch of the
   brakes,
  Though on burning sands they rove.

Lions can but loudly roar ;
But the war-cries of the Eagles, when they grapple
   with their prey,

Seem unearthly shrieks, that startle on the timid
    ear of day, —
Frighting even while they soar.

Listen to the hoarse-like words,
That from the hills of old Vermont, in steady
    streams doth come,
Like the deep and willing thunder of many a thou-
    sand drum,
Or the clank of million swords.

Shouts start up in the East,
From Maine to Pennsylvania, they know no pause
    or rest,
Subsiding never, till they find the gorges of the
    West,
And in golden revels feast!

Come they in the winds at night,
From the forest all alive, with the ready forms of
    men,
Who but hear them uttered once echoed from the
    throngéd glen,
When each shouts with mad delight!

From many a future rout,
Where the war shrieks drown the voices of the
    brave men in command ;

In the death tones of the wounded, which resound
     throughout the land,
  I can hear the fearful shout!

From the top of lofty mast,
It is branded on the ears of the terror stricken
     night,
Till the steal-enbearded Lion, shrinks in terrible af-
     fright,
  From the mighty blast!

On many a bright sea wave
In the thunderbolts of iron, from the glistening can-
     non sent,
Which burst into the bulwarks, with such a mur-
     derous rent,
  That each wave, becomes a grave!

From many a brazen mouth,
It will speak in greedy tones, of our unappeased
     might,
Till the clouds of dingy smoke, make the day re-
     semble night,
  Starting from the North and South!

From the white of gleaming camp,
Whether on the inland plain, on the forest crested
     shore.

Or upon the mountain slopings, near the ocean's
  steady roar,
 It is echoed in the tramp !

 Comes it in the clashing steel,
That the stern, and rock-browed soldiers, in all
  their strength hold forth,
As on they come quick thronging, with the spirit of
  the North,
 To make their foeman reel !

 It is sung out in our homes,
And the children take it up, lisp it out, from their
  tongues,
While the sturdy parent heaves it, from his deep
  and hearty lungs,
 " Death to England if she comes ! "

Death to England if she comes !
Over every inch of land, every river, rock, or glen,
Are those thrilling words now heard, again, and
  o'er again,
 Death to England if she comes !

Death to England if she comes !
Battle banners are preparing, trumpet notes will
  soon resound,
And where'er a flag is planted, the hosts will
  gather round,
 Shouting " woe to England if she comes ! "

Northmen ! leave your cherished homes !
Northmen ! gather in your strength, and grasp your
      rifles tight,
Let the cry that leads ye on, in the tumult of the
      fight
    Be " death to England if she comes."

Remember Lundy's Lane !
Though no Scott is with you now to lead you sol-
      diers forth,
Ye have a young McClellan, who will battle for the
      North,
    Oh ! each word of his sustain !

Death to England if she comes !
With her ships of War to batter, and her cannon
      to assail,
And with all her heated wrath, deluges of leaden
      hail,
    She plunges on our homes !

The sullen roar is heard,
Ere the missile, reaches aught 'gainst which it may
      be aimed,
So, this shout, a warning voice, now rightfully is
      named,
    Of a sleeping form disturbed !

The Indian, at the mound
Of a slaughtered comrade, vows a retaliative strife,

And leaping through the woods, he bears the mur-
      derous knife,
  And whets it on the ground!

  So, England! be not dumb
To the voices which I hear, no matter where I turn,
Which say " beware thee England" in living words
      that burn,
  So death to ye if ye come!

  I've been ready with my voice
While the civil war was waged, but some power
      courage gave,
Come Thou! and my form I lose me, in the battles
      of the brave, —
  I shall have no other choice.

  Northmen! gather from your homes,
Raise those sturdy arms aloft, prepare them for a
      blow.
Verify the shout that's uttered, and the dreadful
      meaning show,
  Death to England if she comes!"

THE FARMER SOLDIER TO HIS WIFE.

I am going, Mary, very soon,
    To leave this lovely place ;
Perhaps I never shall return —
    Nay ! do not hide your face ;
But lift your holy eyes to mine,
    From whence such joys have come,
And let me take a deep, long look
    At my own heart's best home.
Oh, you have been, my Mary dear,
    A gentle wife to me,
And many are the hours spent
    In loving harmony ;
But, alas ! my lovely Mary,
    This noble land and free,
Is warred against by those who seek
    To chain it's liberty.

Though storms, a dullness, — Mary, dear, —
    Will oftentimes impart ;
Yet, for the sake of him who loves,
    Oh, keep a cheery heart ;
Nor sit and brood of dangers
    That he cannot control,

But, for the sake of little Bess,
    Pray bear a hopeful soul.
This rosy bower, Mary dear,
    Our love has often seen ;
Oh, keep it's roses blossoming,
    It's leaves all fresh and green ;
So that when I come home again,
    And glance the country o'er,
I'll recognize the blooming scene,
    The bower at my door.

Our little one ! Oh, gently, wife !
    Take care of little Bess,
And claim each glancing of her eye,
    The trembling of each tress ;
And treasure them within your heart,
    Each word and action free,
So that when I am come again,
    You'll give them all to me.
Then joyful be your heart, dear wife,
    With thought of future bliss,
And holy keep this form I press,
    These lips which now I kiss.
Good bye ! dear wife ; God grant thee strength
    To crush all tender fears,
And give long days of happiness
    For these, our parting tears.